The Silicon Divide
Danielle Nowell

Copyright © 2023 Danielle Nowell

ISBN-13: 979-8-218-22195-9

Printed in the United States of America

Content Warning

1. Death
2. Suicide Attempt

Chapter 1

The rain fell on Trocher like it did many of the days. This wasn't ordinary rain that children would play in and jump in puddles; this was acid rain and would burn through any flesh exposed to it. Artemis quickly ran for cover into a nearby shop, droplets of rain falling on her face and hands, stinging her. Luckily, Artemis wore a jacket and pants so the rest of her skin wasn't exposed. The shop was a stand-alone, small, dingy little place with a small flickering light on and a sign on the door that said: "Uppers not allowed". There was a neon "open" sign on the door, but only the O and the N were lit up and flickered. Artemis entered, and the shopkeeper grunted in her direction.

"The acid rain is falling again; I just need some cover until it stops. Don't worry I'll buy something." Artemis said wandering the few small aisles. Artemis walked by some baked goods and noticed the yoshir sweet bread and decided to pick up a loaf for her parents, her dad had been wanting some.

"Here," Artemis placed the loaf of yoshir sweet bread on the counter, "I'll buy this in the meantime."

"Hmm" grunted the shopkeeper again.

Inside the shop there was a small tv that had the news on. Of course, it was government-controlled news so the objective truths about what was going on in the city were not being told. What was actually going on was the Stellar Shield units were terrorizing the humans, especially the Cogs and in some instances, they were even killed by them, on behalf of the Stellar Consortium. Now on the news, was some story of an Upper and his family. It was supposed to be a feel-good story about his and his family's life, and how good they had it, but it only came off as pretentious and misguided.

"Good for him" a random patron in the store said, "he's living a comfortable life, we should all strive for that".

Artemis thought to herself, "his life is only that good because he was created, literally created out of tech; he is AI. Although I can't complain much about my life, my parents and I have it pretty good. Speaking of parents, my mother will be worried about where I am in this rain".

The rain on Trocher wasn't always acidic. There was a time when the rainfall was beautiful to stand in, as the sky would turn all shades of pink and orange with purple hues, and there would be a sweet smell emanating from the ground during the rainfall. Children would often play and splash in the puddles. That was, until the Stellar Consortium of Mirana IV (the planet Trocher was located on) took control of the government and the "Happening" occurred. Luckily, the acid rain had just stopped. That was the good thing about Trocher rains, it usually lasted only a short time. Artemis grabbed her yoshir sweet bread and headed out towards home. There was a slight chill in the air, which usually happened after a rainfall. The scent in the air however wasn't the pleasant sweet smell that used to exist, now it was a heavy metallic smell that sometimes made Artemis nauseous.

"Mom! I'm home" yelled Artemis as she walked through the door of her parent's small 2-bedroom 1-bathroom home. It was a small quaint little place, with another family living in the other half of the building, with rooms identical to the Xeron's. The Xerons weren't well off, but they also weren't part of the Cogs; they did alright and had just about everything they needed with no want for more. The Xeron's house was on a small strip with multiple other houses just like theirs. They were more like duplexes than anything. Nearby was the local school that all the children, except the Uppers, attended. Artemis and her best friend Cassia Graif, who was a Cog - but Artemis didn't like calling her that, attended the school, which is where they became best friends. Cassia Graif was always tiny, standing only at 5' 2". She had alabaster white skin and fawn-colored hair. Most notable about Cassia's appearance were her ruby red lips and deep brown-hued eyes that were intense and inviting; they seemed to draw you in and never let go. Artemis always felt like the protector of Cassia.

"Oh, thank goodness sweetheart I was worried about you with that acid rain and all; you didn't get rained on, did you?" asked Artemis's mom Gwenvere Artemis Xeron.

"Ah, she's a tough girl, I knew she would make it. Now where is that sweet bread you were bringing back?" asked Artemis's dad Dnaru Xeron. Artemis set the yoshir sweet bread down and took a piece, biting into the sweet cakey bread and savoring the delectable taste, and then walked into her room. She was lucky, she didn't have any siblings, so she didn't have to share a room, and neither did her parents, unlike her best friend Cassia, who had four other siblings in a 2-bedroom house. The youngest sibling, only two years old, slept with her parents in their room, while the rest of the kids either shared the one room or slept in the living room, which was big enough for a two-person sofa and a small box tv. Artemis also felt lucky they were doing well enough to make some minor repairs around the house. Some of the paint had started peeling off the walls, so Artemis' parents told her she could paint the walls with her murals. The faucets also leaked so there was a constant *drip drip drip*, that is until they were able to repair them. Cassia's house was a much different story. The whole building was crumbling and falling apart. Cassia's building had other Cogs living there, so they couldn't afford any repairs. On occasion, a few *sheckles*, or form of currency, would find their way into Cassia's parents' hands, enough for a minor repair here and there, or sometimes just a treat, like yoshir sweet bread. They didn't know that Artemis had asked Gwenvere and Dnaru to help them out. Gwenvere and Dnaru didn't quite know the extent of the wear and tear on the house, but Artemis, who would sometimes go over to Cassia's house to help babysit, would let them know.

Artemis sat in her room doodling on a piece of paper. She had her headphones on and so she didn't hear the knock on the door. The knock on the door awoken

Dnaru, who had just fallen asleep to the news. Dnaru got up and walked over to the door. Outside, were two members of the Stellar Consortium's Stellar Shield unit, or Trocher's law enforcement force. These were AI beings, the Upper's who did work, as they were created for this exact role, they were programmed without emotion to remain impartial and unbiased, or so the humans were told. The Stellar Shields stepped into the house, uninvited, and demanded to see the head of the house's paperwork.

"What's this then? You just walk in here demanding to see papers, won't you tell me what this is about first?" Dnaru said.

"Please, Dnaru, just do what they say," said Gwenvere. Still oblivious to what was happening, Artemis kept drawing in her book. Her drawings ranged widely and included pictures of the Stellar Consortium's symbol crossed out with a big red x and "down with the Consortium", among other drawings of wildlife and architecture found in Trocher.

"We have word that there may perhaps be some seditious behaviors going on in this household. We would like to speak to all the individuals in this household to make that determination. Please gather all the individuals in this household here in the living area." said one of the Stellar Shield.

He sounded almost human, almost. He was polite yet stern, and intelligent, like most AI were. Gwenvere and Dnaru were already standing in the living room, so Dnaru yelled out for Artemis, who couldn't hear with her headphones on.

"In which room is this Artemis? I shall retrieve them."

"No that's alright I can get her. Artemis!" yelled out Dnaru again, this time Artemis hearing something took her headphones off.

"Dad? Did you yell for me?"

"Come on out here sweety, we have some…company."

Artemis was surprised to hear there were visitors, cause Cassia didn't say she was coming over, leaped out of bed and walked out into the living room. There, she saw the two Stellar Shield units and her heart skipped a beat and a chill ran down her spine, she swallowed hard.

"What were Stellar Shields doing in her house?" Artemis thought to herself.

"Artemis. Do you have any knowledge of any seditious behaviors occurring in this household? Please do not lie. We have been created with special lie detection abilities and the punishment for doing so is severe."

"Uh…No, I don't know of any seditious behaviors occurring in this household," said Artemis. The taller Stellar Shield stepped towards Artemis and stared her in the face.

"Please make eye contact with me and tell me that again," said the Stellar Shield.

Artemis stood up straighter, stared the Stellar Shield unit directly in the eyes, which lacked the "soul" often found in humans' eyes, and said sternly "No, I don't know of any of those behaviors occurring in this household".

The unit took a second to process and then took a step back.

"Very well, we are satisfied with these answers and shall leave you to your day. Thank you for your cooperation, and goodbye."

The two units walked out the door, and Artemis breathed a sigh of relief. She didn't realize she was shaking and her palms were sweating.

"What was that about?" Dnaru asked.

"I'm not sure, but it worries me." Gwenvere responded, reaching out to hug her daughter and squeeze Dnaru's hand.

Artemis' parents had been together for 32 years. They met when Gwenvere was 15 and Dnaru was 17 years of age. Of course, Gwenvere's parents disapproved of their relationship seeing as how Dnaru was almost legally an adult and Gwenvere was still a child. Gwenvere didn't care though, she loved Dnaru and everything he stood for. They remained close friends until after Gwenvere turned eighteen, and then took their friendship more seriously and started dating each other. Dnaru was a strong handsome man, with rough workers' hands and a strong work ethic. He was also a great family man, caring for his elderly mom until her final breath, and when Artemis was born, she became his whole world. Dnaru was tall, standing at 6' 3", and had bronze-tinted skin, a warm russet brown color. He had lush thick dark salt and pepper hair and a thick mustache. Though his appearance could be intimidating, he had kind eyes, the kind that were soft and had a friendly glint to them, and they were a striking green color.

Gwenvere was the opposite of Dnaru. She had a very slight build. She too was tall at 5'10" but very slender. She had cool grey hair and piercing blue eyes, her skin fair with cool undertones and marked with sunspots. She had a very warm motherly appearance, her face creased with wrinkles from her years of hard work out in the sun and from just living life. She was one that you wouldn't feel afraid of approaching.

Artemis was a combination of the two of them. She had a tall muscular stature, coming in at 5' 10" as well, with strong shoulders, arms, and legs. She had golden wheat hair, like her mother's before it greyed, and the same piercing blue eyes. Her skin was not so fair as her mother's, but not as dark as her father's, somewhere in between as if the sun had lightly kissed her. Although her skin had several scar marks where acid rain had gotten her. She was a spitting image of her mom's younger self in almost every way. Her name Artemis was passed down to all the females in the family in some way. It was her grandmother's name, her mother's middle name and became her first name. If she ever had a daughter, she would pass the name down to her as a first or middle name. The name itself means "butcher".

*****

In the City of Trocher, away from the Cogs and the Others who lived on the outer skirts of the city, the interior of the city was a high-tech futuristic place that the Uppers, or the wealthy AI, lived in. All the AI were well-off and considered Uppers. Of course, the city center of Trocher is where the Stellar Consortium created the first AI, where the

"Happening" occurred, and where the Stellar Consortium took over the government. Of course, the city center would be where all the AI currently live, and none of the AI would ever be a Cog, or even the Others like Artemis.

Trocher was a prominent bustling place where the Uppers are concerned, but downright dismal when it came to the Cogs, or the exact opposite of the Uppers. The Cogs were those that lived in poverty and struggled in the day-to-day. Somewhere between the Cogs and the Uppers, you have the Others, citizens like Artemis Xeron, a human female, who do okay money-wise and sit nestled right between the two but aren't that far off from being cogs themselves. It was a vast silicon divide; humans vs AI.

In one of the tall high-rise penthouses lived Talin Viltri. Talin was created to be an athletic AI. He had a svelte yet muscular build, was tall, standing at 6'5", and had dark black hair that was long enough to brush his eyes but was kept neat and tidy. He was tawny with bronze-tinted skin, complete with a blue shimmer that all AI had. His eyes, a swirl of golden honey and wheat and striking green, which made gorgeous hazel eyes, yet also lacking the soul in them that humans had. His eyes, like all AI, had an artificial light that shined through them. Talin's parents, or the two people that he had lived with since his creation, were wealthy executives in the city, like most AI were. Basically, if you were an AI, you didn't have to work, or were an executive of some sort, or worked for the Stellar Consortium's Stellar Shield. Those in the Shield unit were mainly created for that position, so only a few other AI ever joined the team. Talin thought about joining the Stellar Shield, only because he wanted to do something, but being an executive like his parents seemed like boring and mundane work, plus he wouldn't have minded getting his emotions deprogrammed out of him. Why did the AI even need executives? It's not like they ever really did any business; they were just figureheads. The Stellar Consortium controlled all the businesses and well, finances were a messy subject. The AI, though they were generally wealthy, did not need sheckles, which was seen as something only the lower classes used. That's probably why the Uppers were so wealthy: they didn't need to spend the sheckles they got, as the Stellar Consortium provided for them, while ignoring the Cogs and the Others.

Talin was getting restless at home, he already had played the piano and violin for a good while and didn't find much else to do. That's why he wanted a job, he wanted to be put to use and do something. Talin's parents had come over. Lucretia and T'evse Viltri were the executives of some business, Talin didn't even know, not that he wanted to, he didn't care. They were your typical Uppers living in the city. Talin didn't even think they knew of the Cogs' existence, why would they?

"Hello mother, father" said Talin.

"Hello son" said Lucretia walking over to Talin to embrace him.

Talin always thought hugging was weird, he didn't understand why they would do it, it was something the humans did, but Lucretia liked the idea of a warm embrace, even though they themselves were not necessarily 'warm people'.

Lucretia and T'evse Viltri were intimidating to look at, as previously stated, they did not have any warmth about them. Lucretia was seen as elegant, sophisticated, and intelligent; all the AIs were actually intelligent. Her look was striking with straight long jet-black hair down to her waist and emerald green eyes. She had pallor skin with a blue shimmer, high cheekbones, and wore a long black dress that hugged her body and accentuated her curves and her thin waistline. Her husband, T'evse Viltri could be described as elegant and refined with a touch of eccentricity. He wore his black hair slicked back and had a pencil-thin moustache. His eyes were like the perfect cup of coffee, warm and rich brown, with speckles of gold that seemed to reflect the world around him absorbing everything with keen awareness and yet at the same time seemed dead. He had a prominent pointed nose and high cheekbones as well. He wore a sharp tailored suit with a high collar, bow tie, and patent leather shoes. If Talin knew what intimidation was, and if it weren't for being his parents, Talin might just be as intimidated by them as the humans were. When, and there were very few times, a human, usually a Cog or the other's, was going to cross paths with Lucretia and T'evse, they often went out of their way to not do so. Most of the time the humans stayed away from the Uppers, but even some AI displayed characteristics of being uncomfortable around the Viltri's.

Lucretia and T'evse were excited when they found out they were chosen to be the parents of Talin. He wasn't born to Lucretia of course; he was created in a lab. The process while complex, is simple to explain. The lab techs create a baby, with an AI brain that is only barely programmed, so it functions as a baby. Once the baby reaches a particular stage, the techs then remove the brain and implant it into a child's body and program the brain even more, so that they will function like a child. The baby's body will then be reused for a new baby. The child then will reach a stage where they will progress to a teenager. So again, the 'brain' is taken out, reprogrammed some more and placed into a teenager's body, with the body of the child being reused for a prior baby who is becoming a child. This process continues until adulthood (what would be considered eighteen to humans) where the brain is then fully programmed, and the adult body is chosen. Lucretia and T'evse were there every step of the way and are proud to say they watched their son grow up. Some AI decide to start 'child rearing' from childhood, or teenagers, some even take on adults. Some AI don't get chosen to take on a child, and some AI who are chosen to decline to do so. The purpose was to have a humanistic society without the shortcomings of humanity. The AI on Mirana IV were programmed with feelings and emotions, but not all of them had the wide range of them.

"How was work" asked Talin, knowing that his parents did nothing all day.

"Oh Talin, you should join us one day at work and see what we do, you may change your mind and want to join us at work" said T'evse.

"Yea well if I want to work, I want to do something, at least the Stellar Shield units actually do stuff" Talin responded.

Lucretia scoffed.

"Why would you want to be associated with them? Sure, they're Uppers like us, but that's a lowly job, wrangling those Cogs and whatnot. It's simply not a job for someone of your caliber and intelligence."

Talin knew his parents wouldn't understand, they were 'brainwashed' by the Stellar Consortium, like most of the Uppers. Of course, it's easy to be brainwashed when your brain itself was programmed by the very people they idolize.

Chapter 2

Back over on Lyxian Lane, where Artemis and Cassia lived, Artemis was going over to visit Cassia. Today was another day where Artemis was going to help with the babysitting. When Artemis got to the Graif's house, she knocked on the door – a few minutes passed before she heard shuffling behind the door. Cassia Graif opened up the door and Artemis gasped. There stood Cassia, with a bloodied broken lip, bruised black eye, cut on her forehead and arm in a homemade sling.

"Cassia! What happened to you?"
Cassia just shook her head with tears welling up in her eyes and stepped aside, letting Artemis in. Cassia's younger siblings: X'ela, Treele, and Astrid walked over to hug Artemis.

"Cassia, where's Arith? Is she with your parents? Where are they?" asked Artemis. Cassia shrugged and started to cry.

"Cassia, what's going on? What happened?" Artemis looked at the other Graif siblings, who were standing around looking solemn.

"They came Artemis, they came asking questions and weren't satisfied with the answers. So this is what they did to me. They were going to take Arith for 'reconditioning', but my parents fought for them not to, Arith is only two years old for Alzarth's sake. How can she be reconditioned? Anyway, they didn't like my parents' refusal of taking Arith, so they took my parents too. They beat them and took them away."

The 'they' refers to the Stellar Shield, and reconditioning was a brutal program the Stellar Consortium devised to 'brainwash' rebellious people into believing in the government. They hooked your head up to a machine that blasted your brain with various wavelengths and literally re-programmed who you were and your thoughts. At least when the AI got programmed there was no pain associated with it, but not for the humans. Reconditioning usually wasn't used on children, as their brains were malleable, and they were often able to be reprogrammed without the machine. Still, it involved taking them away from their parents. Only in extreme cases of sedition and rebellion was the reconditioning program used on children.

Artemis stood there with mouth gaping open. She couldn't believe - or more so didn't want to believe - that the Stellar Shield was capable of such things. She then remembered her own questioning, and how they had told her not to lie as the punishment for doing so was severe. The Stellar Shield units were programmed without feelings and emotions, with the idea that they would remain impartial and unbiased in their jobs, but it also made them cold and heartless, with no feelings to take it easy on the humans. It was a messed up system, thought Artemis.

Then Artemis thought quietly to herself "is that why they came to my house?"

"What?" asked Cassia.

"The other day, two units came to the house, they asked my parents and I about any seditious activity going on in the house. Did you tell them anything?"

"No, of course not Artemis! I swear to Alzarth I didn't say a thing, why do you think my face looks like this?"

"I- I know, I know you would never rat me out, I'm sorry. How are your other siblings holding up?" Artemis turned to Astrid, who was eight years old. "Astrid, how are you doing sweety?"

"I miss my mommy and daddy and my baby sister," Astrid said starting to cry.

"Aw sweetheart come here," Artemis said pulling Astrid into a hug. Treele and X'ela joined in.

"I hate those Uppers," said Cassia, Artemis nodding in agreement. "So, what have you been up to?" asked Cassia, sniffling and taking a seat on the sofa, wanting to change the subject to something less depressing.

"Well, I'm trying to get into that school, the Stellar Institute of Technology and Design (SITD), I want to be closer to the city and see what the Uppers are up to."

"Do you think you'll be able to get in, as a human? Don't only the AI get into that school?"

"Well yes, but they do offer some scholarships to human students, although I don't think a Cog has ever been awarded one, there have been some humans that attended the school. The most notable being Tema Sule".

Tema Sule was an 'Other' who won a scholarship to attend the Stellar Institute of Technology and Design, and while there he studied AI programming. After his studies, he was tasked with creating programs for the AI, and he discovered how to make AI 'grow' like a human and reuse the bodies for the next AI. This was, of course, right when the Stellar Consortium took control of the government, they had created the SITD as a way of showing good will, and also because they wanted to control what was studied and learned. The Stellar Consortium wanted to ensure the students attending SITD knew of the Consortium's power and what they stood for. The Stellar Consortium surprisingly consisted of all humans. They were the one's responsible for the creation of the AI, so even though the AI were the Uppers and looked down on the Others and the Cogs, they followed the Consortium as they were the creators. Soon after the Stellar Consortium took over, the 'Happening' occurred. The "Happening" is to blame for separating the citizens into Uppers and Cogs. Prior to the "Happening" everyone lived pretty equally.

The Stellar Consortium had all AI programmed to be like humans without the flaws and weaknesses of humans, it also gave them power over the others. Those who were poor and living in poverty became known as Cogs. It was a term that was meant in a derogatory way, but the Cogs took the term and made it something meaningful. What is a cog? A single piece of machinery that is required for bigger machinery to work. Many things couldn't run or be created without cogs, as such, the city wouldn't thrive without the human Cogs. Mechanical cogs were also cylindrical but had 'teeth', which the human Cogs took to represent their grit and strength they had.

"Listen, do you want me to spend the night with you all? I'll sleep on the floor, I don't mind" asked Artemis.

"Sure, that would be nice" responded Cassia. Then Cassia asked, "Have you drawn anymore?"

"Yes, I've drawn some stuff in the house, and painted a few things. Of course, I always have my notebook with me which is where I do most of my drawing." responded Artemis, taking a seat on the sofa next to Cassia.

"Can I take a look?" asked Cassia, Artemis reached into her bag and pulled out a tattered looking sketchbook and tossed it to Cassia, who started flipping through the pages. "Wow, these are great. You're crazy talented."

"Eh they're just my doodles."

"And anti-Stellar Consortium stuff"

"Shhh, no one needs to know that. Say, I'm hungry, what do you want to do for dinner?"

"I'm not sure, I don't think we have anything here to eat, and there's the five of us remember." Cassia said looking towards the small kitchen.

"Well how about I go out and get us some food then? You can stay here with your siblings"

"Okay thanks, you're the best"

"No, you're the best," and with that Artemis stood up and walked out the door.

The weather was pleasant, it wasn't too hot or cold, and the suns had been setting. Mirana IV was a binary star system meaning that it had two suns. So, when the suns set every evening, it created a unique and stunning dual sunset. It was pretty fantastic to see, and it never failed to amaze Artemis, even though her whole life had been on Trocher, so she grew up watching the dual sunsets. Artemis was going over to the corner store to pick up some food. The same shopkeeper was working, and grunted in her direction when she walked in.

"Hello to you too," said Artemis. She walked over to the small section of meats, and picked up some Suliyah meat, which was like a ginormous hairy cow. One could get a lot of meat off a Suliyah; therefore, it was reasonably priced, and was the preferred meat of the Cogs and Others. The Cogs usually only bought it as a special treat, since they generally didn't have enough money to purchase meat daily. Artemis then picked up some root vegetables. There was never a shortage of those vegetables as Trocher was the number one producer. The Cogs and some of the Others often spent most of their time working the vegetable fields. They were the ones that had to do it, as the AI wouldn't work the fields; they didn't need to as they didn't need to eat. Artemis walked up to the counter to pay.

"Hmph" grunted the shopkeeper, "twelve sheckles". Artemis grabbed the handful of sheckles in her pocket and placed the equivalent of twelve on the counter.

Artemis started walking back to Cassia's house, when she stumbled upon a group of Stellar Shield units harassing a human on the street. They were dressed in their usual skin tight black tactical uniforms.

"Human, do not lie to us. We are equipped with special lie detection abilities. Are you involved in any sort of rebellious activities against the Stellar Consortium? Do you have any knowledge of any seditious activities going on around here?"

"No, no I swear I have no idea about anything. Please, just let me go" the man said, visibly shaken. One unit took a step forward and grabbed a hold of the person's shirt.

"Hey!" Artemis shouted walking over to the group, "leave him alone."

"Please step back" said one of the units, "this does not concern you, human."

"Well, you made it my concern when you started harassing this poor individual. He already said he doesn't know about any of those activities, so leave him alone. Go back to your city center and get out of our space."

The unit stepped towards Artemis, "What is your name?"

"I'm Artemis Xeron"

"And what is your affiliation?"

"I don't have an affiliation. I'm not a student and I don't work."

"Do you live with your parents then?"

"Yes, Gwenvere and Dnaru Xeron. They are retired now but used to work the vegetable farms."

"Processing." said the unit taking a few seconds, "yes, we already visited your house and spoke to you all. Has anything changed since then?"

"No, I don't know anything just like this guy doesn't."

"Artemis Xeron, you have been put on a list of humans that will be closely monitored. We will do periodic check ins with you. Please stay out of trouble. Repeated offenses may lead to reconditioning. Our business here has concluded." The Stellar Shield units then walked away, Artemis' fists clenched, and she was frowning. This was not good for her, or her poor parents. How would she ever join the Silicone Defiance now with the Stellar Shield monitoring her?

Before Artemis walked back to Cassia's, still shaken by the experience, she checked in with the other man that also had just experienced the Stellar Shield.

"Hey, are you okay? Did they harm you at all?" asked Artemis.

"No, I'm fine thank you. Thank you for standing up for me, most people just walk on by because they don't want to get involved."

"Well, the units can be scary and intimidating, and when you follow the Stellar Consortium, why would you get involved?" Artemis had to be careful of her words, she couldn't let slip that she was against the Stellar Consortium, she didn't know who was listening, or who would rat her out and report her to the Stellar Shield.

"Yeah, you're right," said the man. "Thanks again."

Artemis then walked on to Cassia's house. When she arrived, she was still shaken up.

"Artemis what's wrong? You look like you've just seen a putrid decayed mentrel (a cute small weasel like creature that walked on its two back legs and had thumb like fingers)"

"I had another run in with the Stellar Shield. They were bothering this guy on the street, asking him about any rebellious activity. Poor guy was scared out of his boots. So, I told the Stellar Shield units to stop bothering him. They didn't like that too much."

"Can the Stellar Shield units like anything?"

"Well, you know what I mean. They basically put me on some watch list now"

Cassia stared at Artemis.

"Well, that's not good, especially since…you know…the Silicone Defiance and all that" Cassia said, taking the food from Artemis and heading to the kitchen.

"Yea I'm not sure what I'm going to do now".

*****

Back in Trocher's city center, Talin went to take a walk around. He couldn't stand being around his parents for too long, their incessant talking about their jobs drove him to what he could only assume was the human equivalent of crazy. Could AI even get bored or mad or crazy? Most of the AI were only programmed with a few emotions, some learning the other emotions just to say they had them, but the rest had emotions like happiness. Emotions like fear, anger, and sadness were seen as flaws in the humans and thus were not programmed into the AI initially.

The humans rarely went into the city center, they didn't have a need to be there, there was nothing for them to do. The only exception were those human students at the Stellar Institute of Technology and Design. Even then, most of the students commuted in every day. While on Talin's walk, he came across a group of Stellar Shield units hanging out. Talin walked up to them, "hello, what is going on?"

"Nothing at the moment, just waiting for our next call. Probably going to be some Cog acting up, as they do."

"I see. I was wondering, is the Stellar Shield currently hiring?"

"Aren't you a Viltri? Why would you want to work? And for the Stellar Shield at that?" one of the AI said.

"I just want to do something with my time, but don't want to sit in a stuffy boardroom hearing other executives go on about their finances. I want to get my hands dirty, so to speak"

"Okay, well here, take my card and give that number a call. We'll see what we can do." Talin accepted the business card and walked on. Talin continued walking when he spotted a human walking down the street. "That's weird," Talin thought, "must be a student, she looks awful young though, I wonder what she's doing all the way over here by herself". Suddenly, the group of units he had been talking to ran up and surrounded the human.

"Cog, freeze and do not move"

"Wha – what is this? What did I do?" The girl said, her eyes getting wide with fear.

"Please refrain from moving, and state your name" Talin stopped and watched at the exchange. The Cog probably shouldn't have been over here in the first place.

"My – my name is Jezida Lolen" the human replied. She was a tiny girl. She couldn't have been more than 4' 5" and looked to be no more than 14 years of age, so definitely not a student.

"Jezida Lolen. You have a sibling that was taken for reconditioning, correct? A 22-year-old brother: Razzen Lolen"

"Y-Yes" Jezida said hesitantly.

"Have you continued your brother's actions in his absence?

"No, no of course not. I'm not part of any groups like that. I swear." The girl's breathing became rapid, her heart pounding in her chest, hands shaking.

The units took a step closer to Jezida.

"Jezida, we are programmed with lie detection ability, and the punishment is severe. I will ask you again, are you involved in any of your brother's illegal activities conspiring against the Stellar Consortium?"

"No! I swear! Please, just let me go" Jezida managed to squeak out and started to cry.

"We do not believe you. Due to your connection to other conspirator activities, you cannot be allowed to continue. We do not believe reconditioning would be satisfactory in this circumstance. The punishment for you is death."

"NO! Please!" The girl pleaded, her eyes got wide and all color had drained from her body, and Talin was pretty sure she had wet herself. Jezida started frantically looking around, as if she had any chance of escaping. Suddenly, the lead unit stepped forward and struck the girl, the body of Jezida dropping like a ton of bricks. The AI had landed a fatal blow, which was easy to do when you were machine. The other units surrounded her body. Jezida never had a chance. The Stellar Shield never carried weapons, as items like guns were seen as uncivilized tools the humans used. The units used their hands as weapons, as if that were any more civilized than a gun. The belief of the Stellar

Consortium was that guns removed the person from the act and was easy to use. Being hands on kept you involved and made you think about the action you were doing. As AI, the Stellar Shield units were built athletic-like specifically for the role, and so when they had to kill someone, they resorted to brute force. Talin watched the whole thing go down and got this unusual feeling inside him, one he hadn't experienced before. Did he feel 'bad' for the girl? Surely there was a more *humane* way of dispatching, or killing, a human, no?

"Do not worry fellow citizen, the situation is under control and the threat has been neutralized." One of the Stellar Shield said to Talin.

"What kind of threat is a 14-year-old girl? Surely, she could have been reconditioned?" Talin asked, genuinely curious.

"Incorrect. Her family has strong ties to the Silicon Defiance. She already had a chance when her brother got caught and taken for reconditioning. Unfortunately, it did not seem to deter her from continuing the seditious activities, the tie was too strong, and she was too brainwashed by it. It starts off small, a whisper here or there, delivering messages for the rebellion, and next thing you know she's grown up into a full-blown rebellion leader trying to take down the Stellar Consortium."

"I see." Talin still didn't fully understand it.

"Anyway, if you're still interested in being a part of us, come by the station on 31st at 2:00 pm and we'll see what we can do".

Talin nodded. Could Talin do what needed to be done? Would he have to be reprogrammed to do the job?

Chapter 3

Artemis got up early, brushed her teeth, took a shower and got dressed. She walked into the tiny kitchen that only had enough counter space for a cutting board and a coffee maker. Luckily, they were one of the families that had a decent size fridge, slightly bigger than a mini fridge. Cassia's family had a mini fridge only. Artemis made herself breakfast, she decided on porridge and fruit, which is what she normally ate. Porridge was filling and cheap, the fruit was not so much cheap, but she was lucky they happened to have some on hand. It was a little treat.

"What's on the agenda today" Dnaru asked, seeing Artemis getting ready.

"Oh nothing, just going out" Artemis replied.

"Well, don't get into any trouble. The Stellar Shield have been cracking down lately on us humans, especially the poor Cogs. Make sure you tell Cassia to be safe."

"Don't worry papa, I'll be fine and I'll let her know." Artemis said, taking a bite of her porridge. Artemis finished up her breakfast and left the house, heading towards the train station. When she got there, it was bustling with people going to and fro and some people milling about. There was already a train in the station, but it wasn't the one Artemis needed. Today, she was going into the city. She was going to visit the Stellar Institute of Technology and Design and see about getting a scholarship to the school.

"Dad doesn't need to know I'm going into the city, all he'll do is worry." Artemis said to herself. "One ticket into Trocher city please".

"That will be 17 sheckles" said the ticket agent.

"Come again? How much?" Artemis couldn't believe the price increase.

"17 sheckles."

Artemis pulled out the equivalent of 17 sheckles and placed them on the counter.

"Train will be here in 10 mins"

Artemis grabbed her ticket and walked over to the platform and sat on a bench and after a few minutes passed, there were less people at the station as most had gotten on the other train that was going out to the fields; it was a workday after all. There were only three other people waiting with her to go into the city center. It was cooler out, and Artemis had some goosebumps on her arms from the slight chill in the air. It always seemed more breezy on the platform as well.

Trocher itself was circular shaped, with the main city being in the center of the circle, and the humans living on the outer skirts around the city center. The fields were on the outer edges of the circle and extended beyond. The next city wasn't for hundreds of miles. The humans never traveled to the other cities as the AI did, even then, the AI didn't really traverse to the other cities much, usually only during once-a-year business trips or trips of goodwill set up by the Stellar Consortium.

The train horn blew as it approached the station. Artemis stood up and walked to the edge of the platform, the slight breeze in the air causing more goosebumps on Artemis' arms, even though she was wearing a jacket. The train slowed and then came to a complete stop and opened its doors. Two people stepped off the train, they had been crying – "…can't believe she's gone. Her poor lifeless body…" Artemis overheard the woman say. Artemis felt bad for them, whatever their situation may be; Artemis wouldn't pry. Artemis stepped onto the train with the other two individuals who were waiting. Artemis took a seat by the window and put her headphones on. Even though it was a fast bullet train, the journey would take about thirty minutes to get to the city center train station. The train started to pull out of the station, and quickly gathered speed. The gentle motion of the train was lulling Artemis to sleep. With half closed eyelids, she stared out the window at the passing scenery of houses and long stretches of empty roads (no one had cars; the humans couldn't afford them, and the AI didn't need them in the city). Thirty minutes later, the train started to slow and pull into the city center station. Artemis and the two other people who were on the train with her got off. Artemis had been to the city center once before with her parents when she was younger as part of a project for school, but she was feeling a little nervous this time.

Artemis walked down the street towards the SITD, passing some AI on the way. Artemis felt out of place, and the way the Uppers stared at her as she walked down the street, she knew she didn't fit in. The Uppers, being AI beings, had a slight blue shimmer to their perfectly sculpted bodies and their necks and joints were see-through where you could see the tech in them. Some of the AI didn't wear clothing, the other AI who did wear clothing were always dressed sharply. Artemis today wore black skinny cargo pants, a light gray hooded sweatshirt, a dark grey jacket over it, and some black boots. Her hair was thrown up into a ponytail with her bangs hanging down in her face. She had a backpack slung over her shoulder. She definitely stood out against the Uppers in their suits and dresses, or nothing at all.

Artemis approached the SITD and had a feeling in the pit of her stomach. Why was she nervous? The worse they could do was say "no", but then what? Artemis walked up the stairs and into the building. It was a vast space with cool tones; it almost felt cold and sterile inside. It was gray all over with blue lights everywhere. In the center of the floor was a reception desk, manned by an AI.

"Hello, I am here to speak to the director please" Artemis said.

"Do you have an appointment?"

"Well, no, I don't, but I know he takes walk-ins."

"Very well", the AI said and held up a data pad, calling the director. "Yes sir, I have a…human…here to see you…yes sir, very well sir." The AI closed the application. "Please head on up to the 10th floor, he will see you there."

"Thank you". Artemis turned and walked to the elevator, and egg-shaped capsule that was a high-speed elevator seeing as though this building had 110 stories to it. It was a multi-use space, and the school was mainly located on the 10th floor. The other floors contained labs, and some living spaces for the Uppers who were students at the school. Artemis got to the 10th floor and stepped out. Waiting, was an AI who looked very distinguished.

"This must be the director of the school" Artemis thought to herself. "Hello, sir" Artemis said.

"Hello, and your name is?"

"Artemis, Artemis Xeron"

"Very well, Artemis, are you here to waste my time or is there something I can assist you with?"

"Well sir, I am very interested in being a student here at SITD. I know you offer some scholarships to humans, and I would like to apply for one". The director let out a chuckle, which was seemingly human.

"Artemis. It is a very competitive program to get into. Everyone thinks they are the next Tema Sule. Are you the next Tema Sule, hmm? Do you have something special to bring to SITD? Do you have what the Stellar Consortium is looking for?"

"I – uh, I believe I do have something to offer, and I believe I can get a lot out of this school. We would both benefit from my attending this school. I have confidence in that I am a very bright and fast learner and will excel in my classes, and I trust the classes here have a lot to teach."

"I see." Said the director, not seeming very convinced.

"Please. At least let me put in an application. It's my dream to attend the SITD. You can then thoroughly review my application and make your judgment then."
The director stood for a moment processing Artemis' request, weighing the pros and cons of letting this human apply to the school.

"Very well, I will provide you with the application which will then be thoroughly reviewed. You have one week to fill it out and submit the requirements for it. Good luck. For the greater good".

"For the greater good." Artemis hated saying that. It was a saying the Stellar Consortium came up with to show that everything they did was "for the greater good", as if it explained their heinous policies and oppression of the humans. The AI never really said it among themselves, but they would say it to the humans and vice versa. When Artemis was in grade school, they started every day by saying it as well. One time, Artemis refused to say it, and she got rapped on the hand with a ruler by the teacher. The teacher than spoke to Artemis' parents, but they weren't mad at her. They always knew she was a little firecracker. They worried about her and her outspoken mouth. They just told her that she had to be careful with what she chose to say, or not say, and around whom she did that. Artemis really only trusted Cassia, and no one else.

Artemis finished at the school and left, and started walking down the street, stopping by a café for a drink. She popped into the café and ordered a Sitarine tea from the tablet. They were one of her most favorite drinks. Warm, comforting and delicious. A robotic machine was behind the counter making the drinks, it was a fully automated process.

"One hot Sitarine tea," said the robotic voice as a robotic arm placed the drink on the counter in front of her. Artemis grabbed her drink and headed out the door. She was looking down and hadn't been paying attention when she walked right into someone, or something. "Shit! I'm so sorry" Artemis said shaking her hands from the spilled tea.

"Please, watch where you are going," said the AI, looking at his clothing to see if any of the drink had got on him. Artemis looked up and was stricken by how gorgeous this AI was. He had a muscular build and was tall. He had dark black hair and bronze-tinted skin with a slight blue shimmer. His eyes, oh how beautiful his eyes were. They were stunning hazel eyes. Artemis wasn't one to swoon for AI. She never really liked them and hated what they stood for, generally. Not that it was entirely their fault as they were created, but still, she usually couldn't stand them. This one was different though, he was stunningly handsome, she had never seen an AI like him before. What was this rush of warmth her cheeks were feeling? Artemis was blushing.

"I'm sorry, I wasn't paying attention" Artemis said.

"Obviously. You need to be more careful. You could have run into the wrong AI, and they would have called the Stellar Shield on you."

"I know, again, I am sorry, I'll be more careful". The Upper started to walk away, in the same direction the Artemis had to go, so Artemis started walking behind him. The Upper looked back and saw this human following him.

"Are you following me?" asked the Upper.

"Oh, no definitely not. It's coincidence we're going the same direction. That's all."

"So, I don't need to call the Stellar Shield on you?"

"I'd rather you didn't. That would put a damper on my day" Artemis said while the Upper let out a brief chuckle, both continued walking the same direction.

"Very well then, where are you headed to?" Talin asked.

"The train station, I'm headed back home from the SITD"

"Oh, the SITD? So you are a student there?"

"No, not yet anyway. I was inquiring about their scholarship program. I met with the director who gave me an application"

"Well good luck then, I suppose."

"Do AI believe in luck? I would assume you don't have beliefs?"

"That would be a fairly correct assumption. We do not have beliefs in the sense of human beliefs, but we do have what was programmed in us, so we do believe in things, it's just how we're made. I would say luck is just statistical probability, but that doesn't mean there isn't the random outlier that throws us off. That I would suspect is what you humans call luck".

"Spoken like a true AI".

"What is your name? I am Talin."

"Well hello Talin, I'm Artemis, Artemis Xeron"

"Well Artemis, it looks like this is your stop. It was nice talking with you, I don't get human conversation very often. It's a refreshing change of pace to talking with other AI. You're so…human."

"Gee, thanks, I think. Anyway, it was nice meeting you, Talin". With that, Artemis jogged up into the train station, leaving Talin standing on the sidewalk. Artemis was generally surprised at her conversation with Talin. She actually enjoyed it and her walk with him. It was very different than her usual encounters with AI, especially if they're Stellar Shield.

*****

Talin couldn't make the meeting with the Stellar Shield that day he met them. He had prior obligations to attend to. He decided today he would go and see if the lead unit he spoke with was available. Talin got up from his recharging table (since AI didn't eat for energy, they had recharging tables where they 'slept') and got dressed. Talin, unlike the other AI, usually didn't dress as sharply. It was something his parents always chided him on. Not that Talin cared. Talin didn't feel any attachment to his parents, as AI generally didn't form attachments. Today, Talin decided to wear black pants, with a black button-down shirt and a brown leather jacket over it. He also wore some brown leather boots.

Talin left his house and headed towards the Stellar Shield station headquarters. There were a few stations throughout the city, and some stations located closer to where the humans lived, which Talin suspected were the not great placements that the newbies probably got, or you got sent if you got in trouble. Talin approached the big building with the rotating symbol of the Stellar Consortium on the roof top. The headquarters building was the second largest building in the city aside from the SITD building. Talin walked inside and walked up to the reception desk. Talin handed over the business card and asked to speak to the lead unit he had met.

"One moment please" said the AI at the front desk while she radioed Stellar Shield 124 or SS 124. Of course, the units had names, but most of the time they were referred to by their numbers. In this case, the lead unit, who went by the name Xarius, was called SS 124. Soon, the elevator opened up and out stepped the SS unit. He was a big guy; most of the AI were all tall. He was very muscular with big broad shoulders and thick arms. He looked different than most of the AI who had slender, thin builds, or athletic but not overly muscular builds. Talin could see why he was the lead.

"Hello, I am sorry, I do not believe I ever got your name; we met the other day on the street, you gave me your business card."

"Yes, welcome. I'm Stellar Shield unit 124 but you can call me Xarius." Xarius stuck his hand out to Talin, Talin reciprocated.

"I have come to see about applying for the Stellar Shield."

"Yes, yes, that's right you had mentioned that before. Well, come, take a walk with me and I'll explain a little about the process and what we do, and you can decide if that's still something you'd like to join." Xarius headed back towards the elevator.

"Xarius, how many AI are actually on the force?"

"Let's see, we currently have 1,250 on the force, but obviously not all work at the same time. We work three days on three days off and it rotates through everyone."

"1,250? That seems like a whole lot for this city, no?" Talin asked.

"Well when you think about it, each station has to be fully staffed in the city, and then there are those stations by the humans' living locations which also need to be fully staffed, plus you have the roaming patrols as well. There is also a morning, evening and night shift."

"I see."

"Up here you'll see squad Bravo hanging out in the break room. They'll usually hang out here until something comes in. Generally, the roaming patrols take care of whatever situations arise on the streets first and only if something comes into the station will the squad react."

"So, are you part of the roaming patrol, since I saw you on the street the other day?"

"No not technically. I'm the lead unit so I take part in all roles, that day just happened to be my day to join the roaming patrol. If I'm in the station and there's a big incident that occurs, then I'll respond out. I also give the okay if any dispatching of the humans need to be done, or if a human needs to be taken for reconditioning, or on the rare occasion an AI needs to be reprogrammed."

"Speaking of reprogramming, would I need to be reprogrammed to be in the Stellar Shield? Since I currently have some emotions and feelings."

"Yes, you would go through our reprogramming class. That would be the first step, to rid you of any feelings or emotions you might have. Our goal is to make you completely unbiased and objective for any situation you might encounter. After, you attend a course to see how we do things, how we respond to various situations and how to dispatch a human if the need arises. I'm sure you saw what happened on the street the other day with that young human girl"

"Yes. Do you dispatch humans often and why call it dispatch and not kill?"

"We don't *kill* many humans; most get off with warnings or the very most reconditioning. Only in extreme circumstances where we believe even reconditioning won't be enough to change the thoughts and behaviors do we take out the humans. We use the word dispatch rather than kill because we think it sounds more sterile and efficient; it's not like we go out looking to kill the humans, we're just doing our jobs."

"Wouldn't using a gun be more sterile and efficient too though, rather than just your hands?"

"Ah but with guns, the humans used to use them often, even amongst themselves. It was easy for them to be on the other end of the gun and pull the trigger. It removed them from the experience of taking a life. The Stellar Consortium banned all weapons because they wanted to have a more refined society. While fighting someone with your hands seems more primitive, the views are that weapons are primitive and unyielding. A human might have a second thought when using their hands on someone. The same rules thus applied to the AI. No weapons. Not that we need them anyway against the humans. Have you ever seen a human try to fight an AI?"

"I can imagine it is not pretty. The humans probably don't stand a chance against you."

"No, they really don't. So anyway, that brings me to my next question. Do you think you can do what needs to be done? The Cogs really get out of line sometime and you might have to handle them."

"Yes, I believe so, especially after I attend reprogramming and the classes."

"Very well. In that case, here is the link to the application. Go ahead and fill it out, make sure you mention my name as Stellar Shield unit 124 on it, so it'll expedite your application."

"Sounds good, thank you. Nice seeing you again."

"Nice to see you, looking forward to working with you." SS 124 said and turned to walk away. Talin looked at the application, but decided he wouldn't fill it out just yet, he was still on the fence about actually joining. Talin left the building and started walking towards the direction of home when suddenly someone walked right into him, spilling her tea.

"Please watch where you are going" Talin stated as he looked down, checking to see if anything was spilled on him.

Ah, it was a small-ish human girl, though she was tall among the human standards. She was very pretty though, Talin thought. Talin usually never minded the humans, much less thought of them as pretty or beautiful, but this one was different. She had a tall muscular stature, with strong shoulders, arms, and legs. She had golden wheat hair, piercing blue eyes like the oceans of Mirana IV. Her skin was not so fair but almost as if the sun had lightly kissed her. The girl had some red in her cheeks as she apologized. Talin warned her that she could've had the wrong AI who might have called the Stellar Shield on her. The human girl was very apologetic.

"Very well, have a good day" Talin said as he started to walk away, only to notice the human girl was following him. "What does this girl want, do I have to call the Stellar Shield on her?" Talin thought to himself.

"I'm headed towards the train station." the girl said. In their brief conversation, Talin picked up that the girl was funny, quick-witted and sarcastic. Talin appreciated that about her, most humans were stiff and nervous around AI.

"What is your name? I'm Talin"

"Artemis, Artemis Xeron".

They had approached the train station and said their goodbyes. Talin was left standing on the sidewalk. He rather enjoyed his conversation with Artemis. It was different than his usual conversation with other Uppers. Was Talin smirking? Talin continued his walk home, he'd have to be sure not to mention this to his parents, who were adamantly against the humans. According to them, the humans were a disease on this planet and should be exterminated.

Chapter 4

Artemis arrived back home from her journey into the city and to the SITD. She thought it was a very productive trip, and she was thinking about the AI she had just met, Talin. She couldn't wait to tell Cassia everything. She called her up, "Hey, Cassia! Are you busy? Can I come over? I have tell you about my trip into the city."

"Sure, I have some important news for you as well that I think you'll want to hear".

Artemis headed over to Cassia's house. Cassia's parents and little sister were still missing, Cassia started to think she would never see them again.

"Hey Cassia"

"Hey Artemis, come on in."

"Your parents and Arith still gone?"

"Yes, I haven't heard a word from them or about them. I'm starting to wonder if they'll ever come back.

Depending on how deep the reconditioning was, they might have forgotten their lives and us altogether."

"Oh Cassia, I am so sorry" Artemis said giving Cassia a hug.

"It's okay, we've been managing. Anyway, tell me about the city, how was it?" taking a seat on the sofa and motioning for Artemis to join her.

"That's right you never been into the city huh? We'll have to go sometime just so you can see it. It's really quite something, it's amazing to see."

"How was the SITD?"

"It went great, I got an application for the school, so I am so excited to fill it out and apply."

"That's great Artemis. Well, tell me about the city, then. What is it like?" Cassia asked, closing her eyes so she could picture the city as Artemis described it.

"The city is huge, and it's such a mesh between technology and modernity. The cityscape is filled with towering skyscrapers made of sleek and innovative materials, and the transportation is dominated by the high-speed trains. It took me thirty minutes to get to the city. Everywhere you look were screens displaying vivid lifelike images and augmented reality overlays. The infrastructure of the city is highly advanced with renewable energy sources and sustainable technologies powering everything. The air is so clean."

"Wow sounds amazing, and nothing like how it is out here in the outerskirts"

"It is, if only it weren't only for the Uppers. We would never have something like that here on the outskirts of Trocher, and we would never be allowed to live there in the city," Artemis said.

"So, I have some news for you" Cassia said, "regarding the Silicon Defiance" Cassia lowered her voice.

"Oh," Artemis said raising an eyebrow, "what is it?"

"They have a meeting coming up. There is a password to get in which is 'The Consortium goes down'. It'll be in the home of Jinx Jablan, do you know where that is?"

"Yes, I know his home. Do you think I could go and get in? They don't really know me, and I don't know who all is part of it, which makes me a little nervous."

"I'm sure it'll be fine, just make sure you say the password"

"How did you find out about this anyway? You should be careful especially with your parents and all".

"Don't worry about it, I'll be fine. I can't give away my secrets or I might stop getting info," Cassia said.

"Alright, I just don't want to see anything happen to you. You're my best friend and the only person I trust. Speaking of trust, though this is kind of random, but I ran into an Upper in the city. Like I literally walked right into him because I wasn't paying attention." Artemis said, slightly embarrassed.

"Oh no, were you okay? He didn't call the Stellar Shield on you, did he?"

"No, I think he wanted to when I started following him though"

"Wait what do you mean followed him? Artemis, you'll get yourself in trouble you know"

"No, it's not like that, we coincidentally were walking the same direction. He did not call the Stellar Shield on me. He was actually nice; we had a pleasant conversation. It was kind of weird. I'm not used to that kind of interaction with the Uppers, especially if they're Stellar Shield".

"Alright, so what did he look like?"

"He was pretty handsome, one of the better-looking Uppers I have ever seen. He had an athletic build, dark hair and gorgeous hazel eyes.

"Well good, I'm glad you had a good experience in the city and with the Uppers. So, are you going to apply for SITD?"

"Definitely. I know I can get in. Then I'll be much closer to the Uppers and maybe the Silicon Defiance could use me then. Anyway, it's getting late and looks like acid rain is on the horizon, I better get home before mama and papa start to worry."

"Alright, it was good seeing you. Take care." Cassia said.

Artemis walked out the door. There was a peculiar scent in the air that usually preceded the acid rains. It almost smelled metallic. The skies were a pink orange color as the suns were setting but since the rains were coming there was a dark purple tinge to the sky.

"Hey mama, papa, I'm home"

"Oh thank goodness, I saw the rains were coming so I was worried about you being out there. Where were you, at Cassia's? How is she and the other kids doing?

"Oh mom, you're always worrying about me. But yeah, I was visiting her, I was telling her about my tri– my drawings, yea I was telling her about my ideas for new drawings. She and X'ela, Treele and Astrid are doing okay, as good as they can be. They said they haven't heard from their parents or anything about them yet."

"What a shame, I can't believe the Graif's got taken, they seemed like such nice people. I don't know how they got caught up in anything. Cassia isn't involved in anything is she? Does she know anything about the Silicon Defiance?"

"Umm I'm not sure ma, I really don't know, she hasn't said anything to me about it."

"Well just be careful and don't go getting yourself mixed up in anything. I care about you and don't want to see you get hurt, or worse."

"Don't worry ma, I'll be safe, I promise"

"Okay, love you to the moons and back" Gwenvere said.

"Love you to the moons and back". Artemis responded.

Artemis went to her room. She didn't like lying to her parents, but it was for their own benefit and safety that they didn't know about Artemis' desires to be part of the Silicon Defiance and attempt to take down the government. Luckily, they never looked in her drawing notebook or they would've seen the anti-Stellar Consortium drawings and would have been very worried about her. Not that her parents fully supported the government, but they wouldn't have wanted Artemis to be as open and vocal about her dislike of them as she was. They would have made her burn her drawings. Artemis would have to sneak out to attend the Silicon Defiance meeting at Jablan's house. Artemis waited for the sun to go down, and for her parent's bedroom door to close before she pried open her bedroom window. It usually was sticky, and she had to use some force to open it. Artemis hoped her parents wouldn't hear the window. Artemis got it opened then waited a few minutes to see if her parents were going to walk in, if anything she would say her room was stuffy and she wanted some fresh air. It had finished raining the acid rain and there was a rare freshness to the air instead of the metallic smell. Artemis grabbed her backpack and slung it over her shoulder than crawled out of her window. Artemis dropped a few feet to the ground below landing with a soft thud in some mud that made a soft squishing noise. Artemis paused again to hear if her parents were disturbed and if they were roused by the noise. No one came to her room, so she was clear to go. Artemis started walking towards the home of Jinx Jablan when she walked by two patrol Stellar Shield units doing their nightly routine of patrolling the streets.

"Shit, okay, act normal" Artemis thought to herself. "Hello units" Artemis said to them.

"Good evening human. Whereabouts are you headed to?"

"Just taking an evening stroll, the weather is nice after that rain we had so I wanted some fresh air."

"And what is your name?"

"…Artemis"

"Artemis what?"

"Xeron. Artemis Xeron."

"Artemis Xeron. You are on our watch list in which your responses require extra scrutiny. So I will ask again, where are you headed to?"

"I told you, I'm just out for an evening walk. The weather is pleasant, and I just needed some fresh air, not the stale dusty air in my room." The scent was rather pleasant surprisingly, normally the heavy metallic smell after the acid rains made Artemis nauseous, but the metallic smell wasn't heavy right now.

"Very well. Do not stay out too late. We have word of a rebellion meeting going on, and we have enacted a curfew. You do not want to be caught out past curfew, the consequences are…." The unit hesitated for a moment, "severe."

"Very well, noted. Thank you, fellas."

"Carry on" the units said, and they marched off.

"Crap!" Artemis thought to herself, "That was close. I have to warn the other members of the Silicon Defiance that the Stellar Shield is on to them." Artemis took off on a jog and arrived at the small ramshackle house and knocked on the door. *Knock knock.* The door opened a small crack and a man appeared. He was a big guy with a stocky build, his eyes squinted and covered by thick black eyebrows and a thick black mustache covering his mouth. He asked in a gruff voice "'oo is it?"

"Uh Artemis? Artemis Xeron?"

"Yea what can I do for ye?"

"I'm here for the…" Artemis lowered her voice, "meeting".

"Password?" the man, who Artemis took to be Jinx Jablan, asked.

"Darn, what was that password again?" Artemis thought to herself. She took a minute to think about it when it finally clicked: "The Consortium goes down!"

"Shhh! Keep yer voice down would ye, ye want to get us in troubles?"

"Sorry, no definitely not." Artemis said.

The man opened the door a crack more and peered outside, glancing left and right before stepping aside to let Artemis in. Inside the small little place were ten other people packed in, it was rather cramped.

"This is it? This is the Silicon Defiance?" Artemis asked, not really knowing what she expected. The man with the gruff voice chuckled.

"First time huh?" someone else asked, one of Artemis' neighbors.

"Yes, actually, I just caught wind of this and wanted to join. It's my very first meeting." Artemis responded.

"Well, as you can see, we're tight on space here, so not everyone could fit. We rotate meeting spaces and who joins in on the meetings. Sometimes there's more room so there's more people. Those are for what we call the 'critical' meetings. These meetings like today aren't as critical to the mission, so not everyone needs to attend. Also, not everyone can always attend every meeting. So, long answer to your short question, no, this isn't everyone," another member said.

"I see. Well listen, on my way here I ran into two Stellar Shield units doing their night patrol. Don't worry, I wasn't followed. Anyway, they said that they got word of this meeting going on tonight and that they enacted a curfew, and no one will want to be caught during curfew. That probably means that they'll think you are a part of the Defiance and send you to be reconditioned."

"Oh no" said someone else.

"Artemis, are ye sure ye wasn't followed?" Jinx, the man with the gruff voice, asked.

"I promise. I was sneaky and stealthy on my way over."

"Very well, we shall end this meeting now then. Don't worry Artemis, you didn't miss much tonight. Next meeting we'll go over everything and fill you in, but we can't risk it tonight. Alright everyone, clear out, but remember, to space out your leaving so it doesn't look suspicious. Artemis if you don't mind staying behind just a minute"

"Sure. Of course."

"So, being new to the team and all, do you have any skills or anything that can benefit us in anyway? If not that's okay, we can find a role for you of course, but it helps to know what you bring to the table."

"Well, I'm applying to SITD, I figured if I get closer to the city center, I can keep a better eye on the Uppers and Stellar Shield. Plus, I can see what they're

65

teaching at the school and pass it along. Also, I'm really good at being sneaky and light on my feet."

"That works. We don't really have anyone in the city center or at the school so it would be good to have you there. Very well, you better get going, don't want to be caught during the curfew."
Artemis took her leave. On her walk home she passed the same two units she saw earlier.

"Just on my way home fellas. It was a nice walk I was on."

"Very well, curfew starts in a few minutes, better hurry up and get inside."
Artemis hoofed it home, climbing back into her window and closing it with a thud. She quickly threw off her clothes and hopped into bed, her dad coming to her door.

"Artemis? Are you okay? I heard a thud, and it woke me up." Dnaru said.

"Yes dad, I'm fine, I just had my window open for some fresh air, but I closed it."

"Okay, goodnight sweety, love you"

"Goodnight, love you back"

"Whew, that was a close one" Artemis thought.
Artemis then pulled out her notebook, and wrote some notes down, and quickly sketched some more pictures.

Then she put her notebook away and pulled out the application to SITD, and she started to fill it out. This was going to be how she took down the Consortium, by starting from the inside. After she had filled out the application, she laid down to go to sleep, except she wasn't sleepy, she was energized by having attended her first Silicon Defiance meeting, even if she didn't get anything from it, and from applying to the Stellar Institute of Technology and Design.

*****

Meanwhile, back in the city center, Talin was at home, his parents telling him about their job and how he should give it a shot. Talin had enough when he said "Listen, I know you want me to join you both in your job but that isn't for me. I have an application to join the Stellar Shield, and I think I'm going to apply"

"What? Talin, you know how we feel about that, why would you want to join them and have to deal with managing the Cogs? They're so unruly and human. Besides, you have to go through reprogramming, don't you? You don't want that. What if you forget about us?"

"They don't completely wipe your brain; this isn't like reconditioning. They just take away emotions, that's all."

"But Talin why would you want to give up your emotions? The humans, they're stuck with all of them, but yours are tailored to you. You get none of the negatives of the humans."

"I'm aware, but it's okay, I don't mind giving them up. At least joining the Stellar Shield will give me something to do, and I don't mind dealing with the humans. I -" Talin almost let slip that he had a pleasant conversation with a pretty human today, but his parents were so against humans, he knew they would have something negative to say about it. He didn't want to start with them.

"I just don't know Talin. I don't think you should do it. But you are your own being, so you do what you want".

"Thank you for the support" Talin said. He then got up and went to his bedroom and went to the link to the application for the Stellar Shield. He started to fill it out and his finger hovered over the submit button. "Maybe I will hold off on submitting it tonight and rest on the idea" Talin decided and closed the application.

*****

The next day, Artemis was up in the kitchen preparing her breakfast when there was a knock on the door. Artemis went over to answer it and saw it was the neighbor who had been at the Silicon Defiance meeting.

"Did you hear?" she asked in a hushed voice.

"Hear what?" Artemis responded.

"About Jinx Jablan?"

"No, I didn't hear, what about him?" Artemis asked, looking around to make sure her parents weren't nearby.

"The Stellar Shield raided his house after we had all left, they took him, and I think they were going to kill him. I know you had said the Shield was onto us for our meeting, well apparently, they had more information about the Defiance and that Jinx was a big player in it. So they raided his house to find out more information. Knowing Jinx, they didn't get anything out of him, which probably didn't bode well for him, which is why I assume they killed him. Anyway, we need a new meeting location, and Xara has now been promoted to lead."

"Oh my gosh, I can't believe that. Poor Jinx. I hope they didn't kill him, they could have just reconditioned him, which, death would probably be better for him but it's still sad."

"That's not all, one of the members also got caught being out past curfew. They were on their way home when they were stopped by two Stellar Shield units. As far as I'm aware they took him in, he will probably be reconditioned if not killed."

"That's horrible."

"It is unfortunate."

"Speaking of meetings though, where are the meetings going to be held at now? What about the other locations?"

At that moment, two stellar shield units walked by the house on their patrol, so Artemis and the neighbor ceased talking and lowered their eyes until the two passed.

"No, it's too risky with how much Stellar Shield knows apparently, we need all new locations, which leads me to ask…" the neighbor peered into Artemis' house and looked around.

"Oh no, no no no, no. We cannot use my house as a meeting place. My parents have no idea of my involvement with the Silicon Defiance and my anti-Stellar Consortium views. I won't get them involved in it. No. Sorry."

"Very well. As you wish. I shall keep you updated then on the new meetings. Say, how'd you find out about the other meeting in the first place?"

"I can't say, my source has a source, and I can't risk them getting caught"

"I see, well then maybe they'll let you know of the new locations. Keep an ear out." Artemis' neighbor turned to leave. "Artemis, watch your back, now's the most dangerous time."

Artemis felt a chill run down her back. What did she get herself into?

Chapter 5

Artemis called up Cassia and asked if she could come over.

"Hey Cassia, are you free? Mind if I come over? I have to talk to you."

"Sure, I need help with the kids anyway."

"Cool, I'll be over in five".

Artemis got dressed and left her house.

"Bye ma, bye pa, I'm heading over to Cassia's, I'll be home later"

"Okay take care sweety, love you."

Artemis left out the door and walked over to Cassia's house.

"Hi Cassia, how are you holding up? Any news on your parents and sister?"

"Yes actually, a Stellar Shield unit stopped by earlier, according to them, my parents and Arith are doing okay. Arith was actually not reconditioned, they decided she was young enough they were just going to work with her like on a school level. My parents, well, they have been reconditioned. I don't know how deep the reconditioning went. I also don't know when they're coming back to us, if they come back at all."

"Oh Cassia, I don't know if that's good news or bad news. I mean it's great that you finally heard something, but bad that that happened to them, and you don't know when they're coming back."

"It's okay. I've sort of accepted it, although my siblings are still struggling with it." Cassia said as Artemis looked over at X'ela, Treele and Astrid.

"Anyway, what did you have to tell me?" Cassia asked, while absentmindedly rubbing her arm.

"Oh yes, so listen, the other day I went to the Silicon Defiance meeting. On my way there though I ran into two Stellar Shield units who were doing a patrol, and they had said they caught word of the meeting and they had enacted a curfew, so when I got to the meeting, I told everyone about what had happened, so they ended the meeting right away so we could all get away. Well apparently, the Stellar Shield raided Jinx Jablan's house and took him away. I was told he wouldn't ever give up any information, so they most likely did away with him. Also, unfortunately one of the other members got caught outside during the curfew and was taken in."

"Oh no, that's horrible, you didn't get caught did you? I guess not since you're here"

"No, I did see the two units I ran into earlier on my way back home, they weren't all that suspicious and let me go, and I made it home before curfew. Remember during the 'Happening' when we had an all-around curfew?"

"Yea how garbage was that. The whole situation was garbage." Cassia said.

Prior to the 'Happening' and the silicon divide, before the Stellar Consortium took control of the government, everyone lived happily and equally. When the Stellar Consortium of Mirana IV took over, that's when they started their AI creation, and wanted them to become the superior beings. The humans got pushed to the outskirts of Trocher and they became the poor human citizens. Those that were very poor became known as the Cogs, while the AI became the Uppers. Of course, there were also the 'Others'. There was a curfew put into effect for all citizens, even the AI in the beginning, with the Stellar Shield enforcing it. Eventually, things started to settle down and the humans became accustomed to the new way of life. The curfew got lifted first for the AI, and then for the humans.

"Do you ever think about life before the 'happening'? Before you became a Cog?" Artemis asked.

"Sometimes. I usually don't let it get me down though. I'm fairly content with my life the way it is. I have a great family and a wonderful best friend" Cassia said grinning at Artemis.

"Aww Cassia, you're my best friend. The only person whom I trust. I can't imagine my life without you." Artemis hugged Cassia.

"So how did the application for SITD go? Did you apply?" Cassia asked, while walking to the kitchen for a snack.

"I sure did. I think I definitely got it" Artemis said while taking a piece of food from Cassia.

"So when will you find out?"

"Soon hopefully". Artemis realized she had been getting hungry. "Hey so what do you want to do for dinner?"

"Oh, well we have these snacks. Are you staying for dinner?" Cassia asked.

"Do you not want me to? I can leave if not"

"Oh no, it's fine that you do, I just wasn't expecting it, sure you can stay"

"Well, what do you have? Or should I go out and get something?"

"We don't have much here, sorry. If you don't mind running to the store to get some food?"

"Of course I don't mind. I'll be back faster than a Crespid (a six-leg horse-like creature) can run." Artemis set out the door and headed towards the corner market. The same dingy little place she usually went to, with the same shop keeper who never really seemed to say more than just grunting. Artemis walked by a Stellar Shield who was doing a patrol, but they didn't stop her this time, so Artemis kept on walking. She arrived at the shop and went inside.

"Hmph" grunted the shop keeper, as he always did.

"Hello to you too" Artemis said. Artemis then went to look at the various foods on display to decide what to buy for dinner. Artemis picked out some items and went to the counter to pay.

"14 Sheckles" the shop keeper said. Artemis paid and headed back towards Cassia's house. When approaching Cassia's house, she saw the Stellar Shield leaving.

"Hey, I'm back and I got food for us. What was that about?" Artemis asked pointing over her shoulder with her thumb.

"Oh nothing, they just had some information on my parents is all" Cassia said with a slight quiver in her voice. Had she been crying?

"Are you okay Cassia, you seem upset, is it because you miss your parents?"

"I'll be fine. I do miss my parents but they're doing okay according to the Stellar Shield so that's good." Cassia said.
Artemis stepped up to Cassia and wrapped her arms around her.

"I'm here for you no matter what."

"Thank you. Now, enough of the sad stuff, let's eat, I'm starving." Cassia said walking towards the kitchen to prepare the food Artemis brought.

*****

Talin didn't sleep well at night, not that the AI ever really slept. They sort of went into a state of less consciousness while they recharged on their charging beds. They didn't need sleep in the sense that humans need sleep. For a human, they start to feel the effects of sleep deprivation in just 24 hours of not sleeping. The common effects include fatigue, drowsiness, impaired cognition, mood changes, reduced immune function and physical effects like headaches and muscle aches. If a human goes for a prolonged time without sleep, they start to experience more severe symptoms like hallucinations, delirium and in the most extreme cases, even death. For the Uppers, their 'sleep' was to lie down in the charging bed and recharge, and maybe get their programming adjusted. They viewed sleep as a weakness that the humans had. Talin felt eager about applying to the Stellar Shield. He had filled out the application but did not submit it because he wanted to be absolutely sure that's what he wanted. If he was being honest with himself, the idea of going through reprogramming made him unsure. Not that he was afraid, he didn't have the fear emotion, but he was hesitant. Would he be able to do whatever needed to be done? He thought back to the human girl he had met, Artemis.

"C'mon Talin, clear your head, she's just a human girl".

Talin finally decided he would go for it, he wouldn't have to accept the job if they offered it to him, but at least his application would be in. Talin opened the app for the application and submitted it, his parents wouldn't be happy about it. Talin heard the door open and close, so he knew his parents had come over.

"Should I tell them about the Stellar Shield application?" Talin thought to himself, "no, I don't think I will, not yet anyway."

*****

Artemis and Cassia had finished eating when Artemis suggested they go into the city.

"Right now?" Cassia asked.

"Well, it doesn't have to be right now, but maybe tomorrow? You have to see it."

"I don't know how the Uppers would feel about a Cog being in their city."

"Don't worry about that, you'll be with me. Besides I want to show you the SITD."

"Okay, we can do that then. Tomorrow sounds good." Cassia said, both eager and nervous to go into the city.

It was the next day, and Artemis came to Cassia's house to pick her up. They walked over to the train station, where there were a few people hanging about. There was already a train in the station heading to the vegetable fields. Next arriving was the train into the city; there were only a handful of people getting on that train. Most of the humans didn't have a need of going into the city unless they were commuter students at the Stellar Institute of Technology and Design. Artemis could tell Cassia was nervous, as she observed her pacing back and forth and wringing her hands.

"Cassia, relax, everything will be okay" Artemis said, rubbing Cassia's arm.

"Yea easy for you to say. You're not a Cog. The Stellar Shield has their headquarters in the city. Plus, just all the Uppers that are there."

"You'll be fine Cassia, just trust me. I won't let anything bad happen to you."
The train arrived at the station and a few people got off the train. Artemis grabbed Cassia's hand and walked onto the train. Cassia squeezed Artemis' hand in return and smiled at her, slightly blushing.

"We'll be fine" Cassia thought to herself, "I have Artemis with me".
Cassia always thought Artemis was badass. She was fearless and headstrong, whereas Cassia was more introverted and indecisive; a little on the timid side. It made it difficult for her to take risks and assert herself in the face of adversity, whereas Artemis was the complete opposite. Cassia looked up to Artemis. Cassia could also say she liked Artemis, like really liked her. She often wondered if

Artemis felt the same way about her. Artemis noticed the slight pink in Cassia's cheeks and squeezed her hand back. They sat like that on the train for a good few minutes before they released each other's hands. It was a decent journey, taking about the same amount of time to get to the city as Artemis' last journey. When they finally arrived, Artemis hopped off the train and Cassia timidly stepped off.

"Welcome to the city" Artemis said.

Cassia looked around and was stunned at what she saw. *This* was the city. It looked like what she pictured it to be, a modern tech-fueled metropolis with augmented reality screens and holographic projections all around.

"So, what do you think?" Artemis asked.

"This is amazing. I had always pictured something like this, but I didn't think it actually existed". Towering skyscrapers loomed over some dark alleyways, there were flickering neon lights, and the architecture was a mix between sleek and shiny designs and industrial feel. The city was unusually busy today, with the streets being crowded and noisy.

"So, this is where the powerful and corrupt corporate elite live huh?" Cassia asked.

"This very place. If you walk down this street here, you get to Stellar Shield headquarters, and over this way is the SITD."
Artemis said as she started walking in the direction of the school.

"And over here, is where I bumped into that AI, Talin," Artemis laughed.
Cassia loved hearing Artemis laugh. She didn't hear it often, but when she did, it was like music to her soul. They kept walking down the street until they got to the SITD building. Artemis wanted to stop in and see if they had received her application and if they had any news, she was impatient. Cassia could have done without going into the SITD. She didn't fully understand Artemis' want of attending the school. To Cassia, the school symbolized the Stellar Consortium, and was the cause of where they are now. Artemis walked in and walked up to the reception desk.

"Yes, what can I do for you?" asked the Upper who was working the desk.

"Hi, I submitted an application and I wanted to see if you had received it and what the status of it was?"

"Name?"

"Artemis Xeron"

"One moment", the Upper did some typing and pulled up a holographic info sheet. "Yes, it looks like we've received your application, it's still under review currently."

"Awesome, thank you." Artemis said. She turned to Cassia, "ready to get out of here?"

"Definitely."

They walked out of the school when Artemis saw a familiar face.

"Talin?"

Talin turned to the source of his name. He couldn't believe it, it was that human girl, the pretty one.

"Artemis Xeron?" Talin responded.

"Oh my gosh hi, what are the chances I would run into you again? Not that I literally ran into you this time."

"Well the chances are…"

"No, I wasn't actually asking what the chances were, it was a figure of speech. Anyway, what are you doing here?" Artemis cut Talin off.

"Well I do live in the city, but I was actually headed back from the Stellar Shield headquarters. I submitted an application with them and wanted to check on it."

Cassia felt herself go pale and she swallowed hard.

"The Stellar Shield?" she asked.

Artemis looked at Cassia and then at Talin.

"Cassia, this is Talin, the AI I ran into the other day that I was telling you about."

"I see." Cassia said.

"And Talin, this is my girl Cassia". Artemis said putting an arm around Cassia's shoulders. "So the Stellar Shield huh? Think you'll get the job?"

"Yes, I do not doubt that I will," Talin said. Cassia was still glaring at Talin. Talin leaned over to Artemis and in a lowered voice asked "what is her issue?" while looking at Cassia.

"The Stellar Shield is a bit of a sore spot for her, and well, she's a…well a Cog, so being around Uppers bothers her" Artemis responded, but didn't give the whole story.

"I see. Well, Cassia, you have nothing to worry about, I believe you are in good hands with your…friend, here." Talin said with a raised eyebrow.
Were Cassia and Artemis viewed as more than friends?

"Besides, the city isn't bad, even the Stellar Shield isn't that bad."

"Easy for you to say. Although I am enjoying the city, I've never been here before," Cassia said.

"Listen Talin, can I get your number? I figured it would be good to have an Upper on my side. You seem like a pretty cool Upper, not like the others I have dealt with. It'll be good to know someone in the city when I attend SITD."

"Makes sense. Sure, and it would be good for me to have a human connection. Here is my link" Talin held out his data pad and transferred a link to Artemis' data pad. "Well, I have got to be going now. Nice talking with you Artemis, nice to meet you Cassia."

"Bye" Cassia said.

"Talk to you later maybe?" Artemis asked

"Maybe" Talin winked and walked away.

"See Cassia, he's not that bad. He's rather human, or at least less like the other Uppers."

"Artemis, he's going to be one of *them*" Cassia said referring to the Stellar Shield.

"I know, but I still think he's different than the other AI."

"If you say so".

"Say, how about we stop at this cool little café I found last time I was here. It's fully automated."

"Are you just trying to take my mind off things? But sure, that sounds nice" Cassia said then thought to herself, "it'll almost be like a date".

Artemis and Cassia walked over to the café, which was a quaint little place, as quaint as could be in this futuristic city. Artemis and Cassia walked up to the order screens and placed their orders. The automated robot got to work making their drinks and grabbing their food items. Artemis and Cassia then grabbed their items and proceeded to a table and took a seat. There were a few other people sitting inside enjoying conversation, but not eating or drinking anything.

"I guess the Uppers just like the atmosphere of a café, but don't have a need for an actual drink or food," Cassia said.

Artemis had ordered her favorite, a hot Sitarine tea and a biscuit, and Cassia ordered a regular café hyperbrew latte and a biscuit. They got a booth seat by the window and watched as the Uppers went about their business outside, walking to and fro.

"This is nice," said Cassia.

"Yes, I'm rather enjoying myself. I have great company and my favorite drink. What else could I need?" Artemis said.

Cassia and Artemis sat there drinking their drinks and eating their food, having light conversation. It was getting late and Cassia said "I think we should get going, my siblings will start to wonder where I am."

"Yea my parents will wonder where I am too, they don't know I came into the city. They probably wouldn't be too pleased."

Artemis and Cassia stood and walked out the café, when a group of Stellar Shield units approached them.

"Names?" asked one of the units.

"Artemis Xeron"

"Cassia Graif"

"State your business," the unit said.

"We went to the Stellar Institute of Technology and Design and then we went to a café. Is there something wrong?"

"Negative. We see you are human, and one is a known Cog, so we stopped and are checking to make sure everything is okay."

"Well yea everything is fine." Artemis said.

"Artemis Xeron, are you aware you are on a watch list?" the unit said.

"Yes, I am aware thank you."

"Very well. You are cleared to continue."

"Whew." Cassia said, glad that was over. "I hate them."

"That wasn't so bad" Artemis responded with a shrug. This was the kind of thing that Cassia loved about Artemis, she took everything in stride and never fretted about anything. Artemis grabbed Cassia's hand and started walking towards the train station. Being with Artemis, and holding her hand, made Cassia feel much calmer. They got to the train station and boarded the train back to the outskirts. It was going to be a thirty-minute journey, and Artemis was tired, so she dozed off with the train lulling her to sleep with it's subtle rocking motion and whir of the engine. It was 08:30 at night by the time they pulled into the station. Artemis walked with Cassia to her house first.

"So what did you think of today?" Artemis asked.

"It was rather fun, I actually enjoyed it somewhat. I could've done without the Stellar Shield at the end though."

"Yea, unfortunately we run the risk of running into them all the time, whether we're in the city or not. I'm glad you enjoyed yourself. I better get going before my parents really start to wonder where I'm at. See you later Cass." Artemis said giving Cassia a hug.

Cassia hugged Artemis back, Artemis smelled so pleasantly, she didn't want to let go. As Artemis walked away, she passed by a Stellar Shield unit making his way to Cassia's house.

"Hmm, must have more information regarding her family" Artemis thought to herself without a second thought. Artemis continued home.

"Mom, dad, I'm home" Artemi yelled as she walked through the front door.

"Oh thank goodness sweety, I was worried about you, I didn't know where you were and it was getting late" Gwenvere said.

"Well, mom, I took Cassia into the city" Artemis said, knowing her mother would be worried.

"You what? Sweety, you know I don't like you going into the city, with all the Uppers and the Stellar Shield headquarters being there."

"Oh mom, I'm stopped in our own neighborhood by the Stellar Shield all the time, it's no different than being in the city. Besides, I had to go to the SITD and see if they got my application and what the status was."

"Oh Gwenvere, she's a tough girl, she can handle herself, I'm not worried for her" Dnaru said. "You can handle yourself right, cookie?"

"You got it dad. I handled myself and took care of Cassia, we were fine. Also, I sort of made an AI friend, I think. Well, I have his link anyway on my data pad."

"An AI friend? How'd that happen?" Gwenvere asked, slightly concerned for her daughter.

"We ran into each other twice, and he seemed different than the other AI when we talked. Since I plan on attending SITD, I figured it would be good to have someone in the city that I knew, so, I asked for his link, and he gave it to me, and I gave him mine."

"Well, that's very good sweety, I'm glad you made a friend then".
Artemis then went to her room; she was wondering about the Silicon Defiance and when the next meeting would be as it had been a while. She would have to see if Cassia knew or heard anything about it.

*****

Talin had gone out in the city and was making his way down to the Stellar Shield headquarters. He wanted to ensure they had got his application and to check the status of it. He arrived at the Stellar Shield Headquarters and walked inside. He walked up to the reception desk.

"Hello" he said.

"State your business."

"I am here to see lead unit 124"

"Very well, have a seat and he will be right with you."

Talin took a seat in the waiting area, there were a few other AI sitting waiting, Talin assumed they had reports to file. Usually, the reports involved a human doing something like bumping into them or looking at them strangely. There wasn't much else in the way of crime among the Uppers. The whole premise of the Stellar Shield was to keep the humans in line.

"Ah Talin Viltri." Unit 124 said.

"Hey Xarius. So I submitted my application. I wanted to make sure you had received it and to check the status of it."

"Yes, I was actually just looking at it, it's quite an impressive application, more than most that we see. It's under review by a board now, so I suspect you should hear back very shortly."

"Great. Well thanks a lot, I appreciate it." Talin said and turned to walk away.

"Anytime."

Talin walked out of the building and was headed back towards his home when he heard his name by a familiar voice. It was Artemis Xeron, the pretty human girl, and she was with another girl. They had started conversing and Talin could tell that the other girl, Cassia, was not liking him. It made sense, she was a Cog, and he was an Upper trying to become a member of the Stellar Shield. Still, he enjoyed his conversation with them, especially Artemis. He was happy when Artemis asked for his link to his data pad, it would be good for him to have a human connection. Artemis and Cassia had to leave, so they parted ways. Would Talin tell his parents about his new human friend? Most likely not.

Chapter 6

Artemis was getting impatient waiting for the next Silicon Defiance meeting. She wanted to get more involved already and get the ball rolling on whatever the plan was. Artemis had found out from her neighbor that the next meeting would be tonight. Artemis didn't know where that was going to be, but she knew it wouldn't be her house. The neighbor had previously asked to borrow Artemis' parents' house for a meeting location, but Artemis' parents don't know about her involvement and wouldn't be pleased if they did find out. Artemis felt bad about the situation though because it would be one way for her to contribute to the Defiance, by providing a meeting location. Artemis had an idea, and she went to her neighbor's house.

"Hey X'lena, where is the meeting tonight going to be held? Cause I was thinking, what about that old, abandoned house that's on the corner a few streets over, you know which one I'm talking about?"

"That's actually a great idea, I don't know why none of us ever thought of it. How about we go check it out, and we can hold the meeting there tonight then if it seems like it would work."
 X'lena and Artemis headed out to the house to check it out.

"Looks like rain on the horizon, again, we better hurry." The neighbor said, looking up at the sky that was turning purple.
As they were walking, they were stopped by the Stellar Shield units doing their road patrol. Artemis was pretty used to it at this point, and every time she saw a Shield unit she pretty much expected to be stopped.

"Humans, what are your names?"

"X'lena"

"Artemis"

"What is this? Why are we being stopped" X'lena said.

"It's routine patrol, we stop humans randomly to see what they're up to, it's for the safety and security of everyone." the unit said. "Artemis, you have been stopped multiple times recently. Are you aware that we notate every time we stop you and talk to you?"

"Maybe you should stop stopping me then when I'm just out for a walk. You haven't found anything about me yet, what makes you think anything is going to change?"

"Well, you are on the list, so we are required to check in on you."

"Then take me off the list, problem solved."

"We cannot do that. We are sorry for any inconvenience this causes."

"I am very inconvenienced." Artemis said sarcastically.

"Now then, are we free to go? We're just out for a walk." X'lena said.

"Yes, you both are free to go, have a good night." The units walked off.

"They seemed more polite than usual, that was weird."

"Maybe they're trying a new programming thing to be nicer and more 'human'" Artemis said.
Artemis and X'lena continued walking towards the old, abandoned house. Once they arrived, they were met with a derelict building that had echoes of a past life emanating from it.

"Do you know who lived here?"

"I'm not sure, from what I've heard around town there was a family who lived here, and the father was staunchly against the AI and the Stellar Consortium and so the family was killed on the spot inside the home. They were one of the first people killed by the AI after the 'happening'. The Stellar Consortium wanted to use them as an example of what happens when you speak out against them and make a public display of your disinterest.

"That's horrible." Artemis responded. They walked up to the front door which was rusted over and pushed it open; it was unlocked. They peered inside, unsure of it was safe to even enter, given the dilapidated nature of it. Inside, there were remnants of furniture and what looked like life having been lived there at one point. It was sort of a sad sight to see, a moment frozen in time when one family's lives changed forever. Artemis started to walk inside the house, "be careful" X'lena said. Artemis walked into the living room. It was a small space, like most of the living rooms in the houses here, it wasn't much different from her parent's home or her neighbor's house. Off to the side was a small kitchen, and a back bedroom.

"This isn't bad, I think this could work as a meeting space. We'll just have to be careful that we aren't seen coming into the house and leaving, but if we aren't caught, I don't think anyone will know that we're here."

"Yes, this could work" X'lena said. At the same time Artemis' data pad went off, scaring both X'lena and Artemis, with Artemis jumping back. She pulled out her data pad to look at it, it was from the SITD.

CONGRATULATIONS ON YOUR ACCEPTANCE TO THE STELLAR INSTITUTE OF TECHNOLOGY AND DESIGN. WE ARE PLEASED TO OFFER YOU A SCHOLARHIP TO ATTEND THE SCHOOL. PLEASE NOTE THE START DATE AND ATTACHED REQUIREMENTS WE NEED FROM YOU BEFORE YOU START. ALSO ATTACHED IS A LIST OF ITEMS YOU MIGHT NEED. WE LOOK FORWARDS TO SEEING YOU AT SITD.

Artemis squealed with delight. X'lena looked at her, confused.

"I got into the SITD! This is great, I'll be so close to the Uppers and can keep an eye on things in the city, and report back to the Defiance."

"Oh well that's great, congratulations. That'll be really helpful for us to have you in the city. Are you going to stay in the city or commute?"

"I'm going to commute. No humans really stay in the city."

"How do you feel about announcing it tonight at the meeting? I'll spread the word that this is the meeting location and we'll let everyone know you got into the school".

"Sure, sounds good to me. So, I'll see you tonight then?"

"Yes, tonight, here." X'lena said. Artemis walked over to the front door and cracked it open ever so slightly, just enough to peer outside and see if anyone was around. When the coast was clear, Artemis walked out of the house and headed back towards her home.

"I have to tell Cassia about the school." Artemis thought to herself, "I also kind of want to let Talin know I got in and see if he got into the Shield." Artemis turned down one street and headed towards Cassia's house. *Knock knock* Artemis knocked on Cassia's door, and after a minute the door opened, it was Treele.

"Hey Treele, how are things?" Artemis asked.

"Oh you know, same old same old. Parents and Arith are still gone, although we've been told they're doing well, so there's that. Are you looking for Cassia? She's not in right now."

"Oh, yes I wanted to tell her I got into the SITD."

"Congratulations. If you want, I can tell her for you."

"No that's okay, I'll come back later to talk to her, I have some other stuff to talk to her about anyway." Artemis turned to walk away and noticed Cassia walking up the street followed by two Stellar Shield. "Hey Cassia!" Artemis shouted. Cassia looked surprised to hear her name and looked up with a panicked look on her face when she saw it was Artemis.

"H- hey Artemis" Cassia shouted back nervously. The two Stellar Shield units stopped a few feet behind Cassia. Artemis jogged up the street to meet Cassia.

"Cassia what's wrong? Why are you being followed by these units, is everything okay?"

"Yes, everything is fine, I was just out on a walk when they stopped me, you know being a Cog and everything, so I decided to ask about my parents since I was already talking to them. That's all. Did you need something?"

"Well, I wanted to talk to you, I stopped by your house and Treele said you were out, but I already told him.

Guess what?" Artemis lowered her voice, "I got accepted to SITD on a scholarship."

"Well, that's great, congratulations Artemis." Cassia took a step forward and hugged Artemis tightly. A single tear rolled down her face, but she dried it up before Artemis could notice. Artemis hugged Cassia back and then released her. Artemis could tell something was wrong with Cassia, but she didn't know what, and she wasn't going to pry with the Shield units standing so close by.

"Well Cassia, I must get going, get back home and tell my parents the good news. I'll talk to you later", Artemis reached out and squeezed Cassia's hand, then let go.

Cassia felt a wave of calm wash over her at Artemis' touch, oh how she wanted to rest in Artemis' strong arms. Cassia felt a twinge of pain in her chest watching Artemis walk away.

Artemis finally got to her house where her parents were sitting in the living room eating dinner.

"Hey mom, hey dad," Artemis said.

"Hey sweety, what have you been up to?" Gwenvere asked, taking a bite out of her dinner, tonight it was Muysk with root vegetables.

"Oh, nothing much, just out and about. Guess what though? I have some great news."

"What is it?" Dnaru asked.

"I got into the SITD!" Artemis said excitedly while jumping up and down, "They're offering me a scholarship"

"Well that's great honey, but you know how we feel about you going into the city and being so close to the Uppers like that." Gwenvere said, now rising to fix a plate of food for Artemis.

"I know, but it'll be okay, it's not like I'm moving into the city, I'm going to commute."

"Well okay, we trust you and trust that you'll be okay." Dnaru said.

Artemis then pulled out her data pad to message Talin.

"Hey Talin, it's Artemis, I have some good news, guess what it is." Her data pad dinged with a response, *"Hello Artemis, pleased to hear from you. I'm guessing you got into the SITD? In that case, I also have good news, I got into the Stellar Shield."* The news made Artemis a little nervous, but it would be good to know someone on the inside of the Shield, wouldn't it? What's that saying, keep your friends close and enemies closer?

"That's great news Talin, I knew you'd get in no problem"

"Just as I knew you'd get into the SITD, they'd be crazy not to accept you."

"You hardly know me; how would you know that?"

"I can just tell, it's an AI thing"

"Hmm somehow I don't believe you" Artemis said. She actually enjoyed talking with Talin, he seemed different from the other Uppers; he was almost human, except for his proper language and somewhat cold tone.

"How about you come into the city, and we can meet up and go out for coffee?" Talin asked.

"You're asking me out? For coffee? I thought AI don't eat and drink"

"We don't, but that doesn't mean you can't."

"I suppose. You don't mind being seen out with a human?"

"No, I do not care what the others think, besides you do not seem like most humans. Also, it will help me get to know you better, if we are going to be friends."

"I see, that makes sense." Artemis said. She didn't fully trust Talin, he was an Upper after all.

"Why does he want to know more about me? He could probably access whatever file the Shield has on me and get information that way" Artemis thought to herself, "Eh, he is trying to be friendly, I shouldn't think too hard on it, it'll be nice to have a friend in the city." *"Okay, when would be good to meet up?"* Artemis messaged back.

"How about two days from now? At 10:00 am?" Talin replied.

"Sounds good, see you then"
Artemis was feeling both nervous and excited. This was good for her, she thought. She couldn't wait to tell Cassia about it, although Cassia might have reservations about it just like her parents. "Should I tell my parents I'm going to meet Talin?" Artemis thought, "Nah they don't need to know, yet". Artemis grabbed her plate of food and headed to her room to eat, the smell was tantalizing her taste buds and she started salivating, realizing she was much hungrier than she expected. At that moment, her stomach grumbled.

Artemis also wanted to check on Cassia and see how she was doing. She had to have been home by now and ready for Artemis to stop by for a visit, but Artemis decided to reach out to her on her data pad first. *"Hey Cassia, what's up?"*

"Hi Artemis, nothing much, what's going on with you?"

"Nothing new. Listen, I wanted to stop by, is that okay?" Artemis wrote back in between bites of food.

"Sure, yea I'd love for you to come by, you know I always want to see you"

"Perfect, be there shortly." Artemis responded and finished her meal, then headed out of her room. "Mom, dad, I'm heading over to Cassia's, I think something is going on with her, so I want to make sure she is okay."

"Alright just be safe, those Shield units seem to be doing a lot more patrolling"

"I will be, I'll be home late so don't wait up for me" Artemis said, as she would head to the Silicon Defiance meeting after meeting with Cassia.

"Love you, dear" Gwenvere said. Gwenvere always worried about Artemis, as her only daughter was her whole world. Gwenvere would walk to the ends of the planet for her daughter if she had to.

"Love you too, mom!" Artemis shouted as she walked out the door and over to Cassia's. Gwenvere and Artemis had always been so close, and Artemis loved her mom more than anything in the world. Artemis don't know what she would do without her mom.

Artemis made it to Cassia's and knocked on the door, Cassia answered.

"Hey Cassia" Artemis said while walking into Cassia's house, turning to give her a hug. Cassia hugged

Artemis back and squeezed tightly. Artemis wanted to check on Cassia and see how she was really doing but didn't want to pry too much at the risk of Cassia getting upset with her.

"So, remember Talin? He invited me to the city for coffee, he wants to get to know me better if we're going to be friends." Artemis said.

"Oh really? So, you're going into the city to meet this Upper?"

"Look, I know you don't like him cause he's an Upper, and a member of the Stellar Shield, but he seems different. I'm not really worried about him but don't worry I don't fully trust him. Besides, it'll be good for me to have a friend on the inside, I can possibly find out things about the Shield which might help the Defiance."

"That's true, and I mean you will be attending the school in the city so I guess it would be good to have someone in the city, just in case of anything."

"Exactly."

"Listen Artemis, I know I've seemed off recently to you, I'm sorry for acting in any sort of way, it's just that I -" Cassia stopped speaking, looking as if she was trying to find the right words.

"Go on Cass, what is it?"

"I just want you to know how much I care about you. That's all"

"Aww Cass I care about you too, come here" Artemis said and opened up her arms inviting Cassia in for a hug. Cassia walked forward and embraced Artemis and sighed. This was her favorite, and if she could, she would have stayed in this moment forever, just her and Artemis in a strong and warm embrace. Would Cassia eventually tell Artemis how she really truly felt? No, she couldn't, she didn't want to ruin anything between them, and if Artemis ever found out about Cassia's big secret, the real reason she was acting so off recently, Artemis would never ever forgive her, it would absolutely destroy Artemis.

"Say, Cass, why don't you come into the city with me to meet Talin? I'm sure he'd be okay with it. I think it would be good for you to get out of the house. Think of it like a coffee date for us" Artemis said grinning.

Cass smiled big, "sure, I'd love to go on a coffee date with you, where we just so happen to have an Upper join us."

Artemis knew that would make Cassia feel better.

"We're meeting the day after tomorrow. Now, I have to get going, I have a Defiance meeting. We found a new meeting space, the old, abandoned house where that one family was killed. We doubt anyone will notice that we're there, but shhh don't tell anyone okay?"

"Of course not Artemis, your secret is safe with me" Cassia said.

Artemis headed for the door, "I'll talk to you later, bye"

"Later" Cassia replied.

Artemis walked over to the old, abandoned house, making sure to look around and see that no one was watching, especially the Shield doing their patrols. When she was absolutely sure that no one was looking, Artemis walked into the house. She was the first one there, so she took a seat on the floor and waited for others to arrive. Soon, others started to trickle in, each one checking to make sure the coast was clear before entering.

"Ah, Artemis, good, you made it" said one of the Defiance members.

"Hey Artemis, good to see you," said another member.

"Hey everyone" Artemis said. Artemis' neighbor, X'lena, was the last to enter. She was also now the new head of the Defiance, after what happened with Jinx.

"Hello, everybody." X'lena said, "I hope you all were careful and cautious about coming here tonight." Everyone started murmuring and nodding their heads.

"What do we all think of this location? We got it thanks to Artemis", again the murmuring started, and people were nodding their heads. "Speaking of Artemis, we have some big news that is sure to come in handy in our fight. Artemis got accepted into the Stellar Institute of Technology and Design", the murmuring grew louder and there were a few "what's" thrown in, and an "oh shit" here and there. "Now," X'lena raised her voice some, "I know what some of you must be thinking but listen, this gives us a super close approach to the Consortium since the school was their idea and design. Artemis will be able to keep an eye on the Uppers and what they're teaching and doing at the school"

"What's to say she isn't a spy for the AI and is going to tell them about what we're doing here, now that she's part of the SITD?"

"We can trust Artemis. If you trust me, know that you can trust her okay? I know this is a little scary but it's worth it, for the cause. I've been with Artemis when she's been stopped by the Shield, and they have mentioned that she's on their watch list. She is one of us." X'lena said. Artemis grinned sheepishly; she wasn't embarrassed by being on the watch list, but she didn't want that information just put out there to everyone like that.

"Very well, congratulations Artemis" a member said.

"Yea congratulations" another member said.

"Now to get down to business, as of right now the plan still stands. We will try to take down the mainframe and any surveillance the Shield has. That should hurt the Consortium the most, then we will expose the Uppers and the Shield for what they really are and what they do, hopefully garnering enough support that we can then overthrow the Consortium. Does everyone agree with this plan?" There were murmurings of agreement and heads nodding.

"Very well. Does everyone know their jobs? Artemis we will need you to find out more about the AI mainframe and their programming, as well as the Shield's surveillance systems. You most likely will be able to do that while at the school. Artemis, we will rely on you to help take the Consortium down."

"I can do that, for sure. I might also have an in with the Shield so I'll try and find out what I can without giving anything away."

"That's it then, it's decided. The meeting for today is adjourned. If you have any questions, please feel free to speak to me. Artemis, can I speak with you please?" People started to get up, "remember, time your leaving and make sure the coast is clear". Artemis walked over to X'lena.

"Hey yea, what's up?" Artemis asked.

"Well, I'm the new head of the Defiance, but I need a right-hand man, so I wanted to ask if you would be willing to take on that position."

"Oh well I would be honored to do so" Artemis said.

"It helps that we're neighbors, so we can speak with each other pretty easily. Do you have your data pad? We can link up on there"

"Yes, I do, here it is." Artemis held out her data pad, X'lena linked hers up to it.

"Now we can talk whenever, but it would be better if it's in person, which is why it's helpful being neighbors."

"Listen, my parents don't know about any of this, okay? I'd like to keep it that way, so no mention of this at all to them or around them, got it?"

"You got it, your secret is safe with me." X'lena said as Artemis stood up to leave. X'lena walked over to the door and cracked it open, making sure the coast was clear, two Shield units were walking by so X'lena quietly closed the door and waited a few minutes until they passed. She opened the door again and saw that there was no one around, so she left, leaving only Artemis standing in the house. Artemis was energized by the meeting; she couldn't wait to get started on her role. She also couldn't wait to tell Cassia. She probably shouldn't tell her what goes on in the meetings, but Cassia would never tell anyone what Artemis was up to. Cassia was her best most trustworthy friend, maybe even more than a friend, so it was fine.

Artemis cracked open the door and saw that there was no one around, so she slipped out the door and headed for home. Once home, she quietly slipped inside as to not wake her parents and slipped her data pad out and reached out to Cassia, who didn't respond back right away. "Hmm, maybe she's sleeping, it is pretty late at night" Artemis thought to herself, "Oh well, she'll respond back tomorrow probably, and there's always our coffee date the day after tomorrow." Artemis then got changed for bed, brushed her teeth and crawled into her comfy cozy bed. Artemis enjoyed her bed and she could just lay in it all day if she was able. Artemis was pretty tired she was just now realizing; she laid her head down on the pillow and closed her eyes, quickly drifting off to sleep.

Chapter 7

It was two days later, and Artemis had woken up, excited for the day. It was the day she was going into the city with Cassia to meet up with Talin for coffee. Cassia hadn't gotten back to Artemis the day before like Artemis thought she would've, but this morning, she woke up to a message from Cassia saying how she was looking forward to their coffee date. Artemis thought it was a little weird that Cassia hadn't responded to her message the day before, but figured she might have just been busy or forgot. Artemis got up out of bed and got dressed and brushed her teeth, then headed towards the kitchen to make breakfast. She went with her usual porridge and fruit. Before she got done eating, Gwenvere had gotten up and walked into the kitchen.

"Good morning darling" Gwenvere said.

"Good morning mama" Artemis responded.

"Have any fun plans for today?" Gwenvere asked and Artemis pondered whether or not she should tell her mom about going into the city to meet Talin, but she decided she would go for it, while her mother may disapprove of it, she won't stop her.

"I'm going into the city with Cass, to meet my friend Talin, the AI, I told you about"

"Oh that's right, you have an Upper friend. I don't think I'll get used to that. You already know how we feel about you going into the city, but with you getting into SITD, I guess you'll be going into the city a lot more often now. Just be careful okay, I don't want anything to happen to you."

"Don't worry mom, I'm always careful, and I'll be with Cass." Artemis said grabbing her backpack and heading for the door.

"Okay my love, be careful, love you"

"Love you too" Artemis said as she walked out the door. On her way to Cassia's house, she was stopped again by the patrolling Shield units.

"State your name human"

Artemis sighed loudly, "Artemis, Artemis Xeron. Yes, I'm on the list, I know."

"Where are you headed too and what are your plans?"

"I'm walking to my friend's house and we're going into the city, I'm a student of SITD, check your records."

"Very well, we do see you are enrolled in the SITD. Which friend are you going to see?"

"Cassia Graif"

"Her family has been put on the list too. You are not doing any suspicious activities like conspiring against the government are you?"

"What? No, we're just meeting up to go into the city for some coffee, and to meet another friend, Talin, who is an Upper." Artemis questioned to herself why they even ask that question, would anyone actually fess up to conspiring against the government?

"Ah Talin Viltri, yes, he is a fellow Shield unit. Very well, carry on then"

"Thanks." Artemis said and walked towards Cassia's house. "I wish they would stop stopping me every time I set foot outside my house".

Artemis arrived at Cassia's house and knocked on the door. A few minutes passed and X'ela answered.

"Hey Artemis! Come on in," X'ela said, hugging Artemis as she walked in, "Cass isn't awake yet, you can go into her room and get her".

"Hmm that's weird, she messaged me this morning saying she was excited for our trip into the city, maybe she just fell back asleep."
Artemis walked back towards Cassia's room and knocked on her door. There was no answer.

"Cassia?" Artemis asked, still no answer.
Artemis turned the doorknob, the door was not locked, and she slowly opened the door. Artemis peered her head in and saw Cassia lying in bed, not noticing a bottle of cleaner next to her.

"Cass?" Artemis asked again, louder this time. Artemis walked over to Cassia and shook her shoulders, "hey Cass!" Artemis just about shouted, shaking Cassia. "Oh my gosh Cass what did you do?" Artemis noticed the bottle of cleaner, half empty lying next to the bed. There was a pool of vomit surrounding Cassia's head, and she had foam coming out of her mouth. "X'ela! Call for help!" Artemis shouted. X'ela rushed in to see what the commotion was about, "X'ela call for help, I think Cassia tried to kill herself by drinking the bottle of cleaner fluid," Artemis said panicking. Artemis felt for a pulse, which was weak, and checked Cassia's breathing, it was very faint, but it meant she was still alive. Within minutes, the rescue forces, who were the only team made up of both AI and humans, walked in and rushed over to Cassia. Luckily, they were close by and already in the outer rim where the humans lived. The rescue forces consisted of both AI for their speed, intellect and preciseness and humans for the "human touch"/bedside manner and was the only team in Trocher to exist as such. The rescue force team did a quick check over Cassia and loaded her up onto the gurney to take her into the city hospital. There was no other hospital out where the humans lived on the outer ring, only the main one in the city. It would take about 30 mins to get there, whether by ambulance or train. Luckily, Cassia was stable enough that she would be fine on the ride over. Artemis and Cass's siblings were going to follow. X'ela would ride with Cass in the ambulance, as being the eldest next of kin, Artemis would take the two younger siblings on the train. Just then, Artemis' data pad went off, it was a message from Talin.

"Hey, looking forward to seeing you today"

"Shit, Talin, I forgot. I'll have to tell him I can't make it." Artemis said to herself.

"Hey Talin, something came up and I won't be able to make our meeting, can we reschedule?"

"Sure, is everything okay?"

"I hope so, it's Cassia, she was going to join us today, but now we can't make it."

"Well, I hope everything works out, we can definitely reschedule." Talin responded. Artemis gathered up Treele and Astrid and headed out towards the train station. Astrid had started to cry, and Artemis calmed her down. It was a long train ride for Artemis. She had done this trip a few times already and this was the longest feeling ride she had taken.

Once in the city, Artemis and the two Graif siblings headed towards the hospital. Artemis found herself shallow breathing and reminded herself to be calm for the Graif siblings, who were quite upset with the situation. Once at the hospital, they walked into the reception desk.

"We're here for Cassia Graif"

"Relationship?"

"These two are her siblings, and I'm…her girlfriend", Artemis hadn't admitted to that before, but she was worried if she just said "friend" then she wouldn't be admitted at all.

"Here are your passes, she's on floor 15 room 4301", the receptionist said.

Artemis and the Graif siblings headed to the elevators. When they got to the floor, they stood outside Cassia's room for a moment, unsure if they should go in, unsure with what they would find. Artemis took a big deep breath in then let it out, she slowly opened the door, "Cass?" she asked softly. Cassia was lying in bed, asleep. Artemis walked in followed by Treele and Astrid, who ran up and hugged their sister. Once they let go, Artemis walked over and gently kissed Cassia's forehead and stroked her hair. Cassia's eyes softly fluttered open.

"Mmm what happened?" Cassia groaned quietly.

"I'm not sure, silly, I was hoping you could tell me. But don't worry about that right now, just gather your strength first, we can talk later. Go back to sleep." Artemis said stroking Cassia's head.

"My head hurts"

"Do you want me to get the nurse?" Artemis motioned for Treele to go find a nurse.

"Thank you for being here"

"Of course, dear, I care so much about you, I wouldn't leave your side"

"Oh! I'm sorry I ruined our coffee date, and your meeting with Talin" Cassia said weakly.

"Shh don't worry about that right now, it's all okay" Artemis said still stroking Cassia's hair.

"I'm so sorry for this, I never meant to hurt anyone"

"Shhh, you didn't hurt anyone but yourself. We all love you"

"You – you love me?" Cassia asked weakly. Artemis smiled softly, "of course I love you silly, you didn't know?" Cassia started to feel tears well up in her eyes.

"Oh Artemis, I am so so sorry", the tears fell harder. "I'm so sorry." Cassia cried, both for what she had done, and for her secret that Artemis couldn't know about.

"Hey, hey, it's okay, shhh, there there" Artemis said pulling Cass into a hug. "Don't worry about any of that right now, just focus on getting better and gathering your strength so we can get out of this place, smells like AI in here" Artemis said as Cassia let out a little laugh. Treele came back with a nurse who came over to look at Cass and administer more medication to help with her headache. Treele and Astrid walked over to their sister, "Cass, we love you so much, you are the glue that holds this family together and we don't know what we would do without you, we need you." Treele said.

"Yea sissy, we need you" Astrid said.

"Artemis, you should go to your coffee meeting with Talin, I'll be okay. I'm here in the hospital, how much trouble could I get into? Besides, I have X'ela, Treele and Astrid here with me"

"I don't want to leave you, though. I think I should stay, what if you need me?" Artemis responded.

"It's okay, I'll be fine. I have my brother and sisters here to watch over me. Right guys?"

"Yea" Treele and Astrid responded together.

"Of course" said X'ela.

"Okay, well, let me message Talin and see if he's still available." Artemis took out her data pad and typed out the message: *"Hey Talin, everything seems to be in order now, if you're still down to meet for coffee, I'm currently in the city, so we could meet up, just us two?"*, almost immediately she got a response back, *"sure I'm still available, meet you in twenty?"*. Artemis looked at Cassia, "are you sure you're okay if I go? I don't have to, I can stay here with you."

"And do what? Be bored out of your mind? No, I'm fine, promise. You go and have fun" Cassia said.

"Alright, I'll have my data pad on me so if you need anything, anything at all, do not hesitate to reach out to me and I'll be over faster than a Crespid can gallop. Okay?" Artemis said and leaned over to kiss Cassia on the head. Artemis turned to walk away and when she got to the door she turned back around, "hey" she said, "I love you", and turned and walked out the door. Cassia again felt tears in her eyes.

Artemis walked over to the café and walked inside. She went to the ordering screen and got her usual hot Sitarine tea and a biscuit. She wondered how many humans actually utilized this café for them to stock food in it. It was never super busy or packed whenever she was in there, and most of the time the only other people inside were the Uppers, as again, most humans didn't go into the city except if they were SITD students. Artemis assumed during class time this place was pretty popular with the human students, she just hadn't been at the café at those times to see.

After a few minutes of waiting, Talin walked in and immediately spotted Artemis, it was hard to miss such a strikingly beautiful human. The suns were setting, and it cast a gorgeous glow on her golden wheat hair and made her ocean blue eyes more pronounced.

"Hey Artemis" Talin said walking over to where she was sitting.

"Hey Talin", Artemis responded and gestured to the open seat.

"So, how are things?" Talin asked

"Good, good. How about with you?" Artemis replied.

"Good."

"Good." Artemis responded.

"So…did everything go well today?" Talin asked.

"Yes, we worked everything out and it should be fine"

"And how's school?"

"I'm not sure I haven't started yet; I start soon though and am excited for it. How about you with the Shield?" Artemis asked, taking a swig of her tea, the hot liquid soothing her throat.

"Oh, I haven't started that either, I got all signed up and through the main process, but I still have to go through reprogramming. I assume if I had nerves, I would feel nervous. But alas, I am an AI, so I do not feel nervous. Thankfully. Although, I find myself not wanting to go through reprogramming, I'm going to try and convince them that I do not need to go through reprogramming and my emotions will actually benefit me out in the field."

"That's good, those butterflies in your stomach are never fun to feel, well sometimes they can be if you're excited about something, but other times they just make you nauseous."

"I can imagine that is a discomforting experience for you," Talin said

"Yes, it can be." said Artemis.

"How is Cassia doing? I know she was going to join us today"

"She's alright, there was a bit of an…incident with her, but everything should be okay now."

"Do you want to talk about it?"

"I don't know, it's rather personal and we've still only just met. I don't know anything about you, how do I know you're not spying on me for the Shield, seeing as how I'm on their list and everything."

"That is fair. As an AI I'm not sure what my lying programming consists of but I think I tell the truth only, I do not think I lie. So you can trust me when I say, you can trust me."

Artemis let out a sigh. "Very well. Cassia tried to kill herself by drinking a bottle of cleaning liquid. I'm not sure what was going through her head, or what she's been going through because she hasn't talked to me about anything. I knew she seemed off recently, but I just assumed she had a lot going on with her parents and baby sister being taken by the Shield," Artemis shot Talin a stern look, "every time I asked her what was wrong though she'd just say she was okay, and everything was fine. Obviously, everything was not fine if she resorted to this. Anyway, so then at the hospital I sort of admitted to her that I loved her, I wasn't planning on telling her that or not yet anyway, as I'm not sure what we are, if we're friends or more than friends? I mean I consider her my best friend ever but maybe we could be more than that? She won't open up to me though and I'm not sure why, I'm sure she knows she can trust me." Artemis stopped talking and took a big deep breath in and out. "Whew, that was a lot, I'm sorry" Artemis said after a few moments, she was secretly glad to get all that off her chest.

"No, no it is okay. It is good for you to get all that off your chest. I'm glad you trusted me enough to tell me," Talin responded, "I am so sorry you are going through all of that, and I am sorry for Cassia, whatever it is she is going through. If you want, we can go back to the hospital?"

"Oh, no, I'm not sure she'd want your presence there unfortunately. Don't take that personally"

Talin laughed "I am an AI, I don not think I can take anything personally"

"Well Cassia doesn't like you, cause you're and Upper, and she's a Cog. And the fact that you are now a Shield member, and the Shield took her parents and sister away."

"That is fair enough, I understand. Cassia is very lucky to have a friend, or girlfriend, or just a human being in general, like you. I can tell you care about her very much."

"I do. Just as humans, whatever we are, I care about her."

"Well then you should go back to her and stay with her. We can meet up some other time."

"Okay, sounds good to me, thanks Talin, I appreciate it. For what it's worth, you're not a shitty Upper like some of the others I've met. I actually don't mind you at all."

"Thank you, I think" Talin responded as Artemis laughed.

Artemis's laugh would've set Talin's soul ablaze if he had one, but he didn't, so what was this he was feeling? It was like he started to care about Artemis. Talin did have some feelings, he just couldn't label them, was this what it was like to be human?

"She has someone she cares about already" Talin thought to himself, "besides, you're an Upper, she would never be with someone like you."

Artemis stood up to leave, "it was a pleasure meeting with you Talin, message me for the next time to meet up", Artemis smiled at him. Talin returned the smile and stood up also.

"Will do".

With that, Artemis walked away. Talin wasn't sure but he almost thought he liked Artemis, well he did like her, he appreciated her company and couldn't wait to talk to her and see her again.

"This is weird" Talin thought, "she is a human. Imagine if my parents ever found out."

Artemis returned to the hospital, and when she walked into the room, she found all four Graifs asleep. Artemis grabbed some extra blankets and threw one on top of Treele and Astrid and another on top of X'ela. Then she walked over to Cass, kissed her head again, and pulled the covers up over her shoulders. She then walked over to another chair in the corner of the room and sat down. This is where she'd sleep tonight, so if Cass needed her, she was right there. Artemis grabbed a blanket and settled into the chair, slowly dozing off to sleep.

Morning came and Artemis woke up, all four Graifs were still asleep, so Artemis walked down to the cafeteria to get some breakfast. Lucky for her, they had her usual porridge and fruit. She could've gone with something more exquisite that she normally couldn't eat, like bacon from a Krynnian (pig like creature) or Lekt eggs, but porridge and fruit was calming and familiar to her, which is what she needed in this moment. After she finished eating, she returned to the room to find Cass was awake.

"Good morning sleepy head, how are you feeling?"

"Much better thank you. My headache is finally starting to go away, they're saying I could be discharged as early as this afternoon."

"That's great to hear." Artemis said. Artemis then motioned for Cassia to scooch over in bed and crawled up next to her. Artemis wrapped her arm around Cass, and Cassia nestled into Artemis, and there they stayed, not saying a word, for quite some time. In that time, X'ela, Treele, and Astrid had woken up and gone to get breakfast. The nurses soon came in after to check on Cassia, the doctor had cleared her for discharge. Cassia got up out of bed, slightly wobbly, Artemis reached out and held onto Cassia until she regained her footing. Artemis then helped Cassia pack up her items, and they all headed downstairs and out to the train station.

"Goodbye, Cassia Graif, I hope your quality of care was exquisite" said the receptionist as they walked out the doors.

"Yea, sure" Cassia said and walked out.

"How was your care here, I didn't even think to ask?"

"It was good actually, I was surprised, I didn't think they would be caring for a Cog here in Upper central, but they took great care of me."

"Well that's good," Artemis said. They finally reached the train station and waited for their train to arrive. They only waited about eight minutes when it came. Artemis, Cassia, X'ela, Treele and Astrid all boarded the train and headed back home.

Chapter 8

A few weeks had passed, and Cassia seemed to be doing better, although she still seemed like she was hiding something; Artemis didn't press her about it. They also still hadn't talked about their relationship and what they were or weren't. Artemis was also still attending the few various Silicon Defiance meetings, and she was about to start school the very next day.

"Are you nervous for school to start tomorrow?" Cassia asked, preparing food for her and Artemis.

"A little, but I'm also excited." Artemis said passing Cassia a plate.

"I bet. You'll be great though; you're going to be fine."

"Will you be okay, with me being in the city so often, I won't be close by to you if you need me." Artemis was a little worried about being so far away from Cassia.

"Artemis. I'm not a baby, I don't need you hovering over me, okay? What happened was just a mistake on my part, I was overwhelmed what with my parents and everything but everything is okay now, I'm fine, I promise. It'll be okay."

"I'm sorry, I just worry about you, I didn't mean for you to take it the wrong way."

"I didn't take it any kind of way, I'm just saying, I can take care of myself, I'll be fine." Cassia snapped.

"Okay then." Artemis didn't want to push any further, but she really was worried about Cassia, she still seemed to be acting a little off. Was it time they talked about their relationship?
Artemis took a deep breath, walked up to Cassia, grabbed both of her hands and said "Cassia? What are we?"

"What do you mean?" Cassia asked, confused by what Artemis meant.

"I mean, what is our relationship? Are we just best friends, or are we more than friends? You already know how I feel about you, that I love and care about you. What do you feel?" Artemis asked. Artemis could feel her heart pounding in her chest, her hands getting a little bit sweaty. Cassia wasn't sure what she should say. She too loved and cared for Artemis, but she wasn't sure she wanted to say it out loud. That would make it real, and sometimes real was scary. "I – you mean a lot to me, Artemis, I look up to you and admire you" Cassia said.

"But you don't feel the same way about me as I do you?"

"No, no, it's not like that it's just – getting attached is hard. And I don't want to see any one of us get hurt."

"Well, sometimes hurt is a part of life. You can't avoid everything all the time for fear of getting hurt." Artemis said as Cassia sighed.

"That. That right there is why I love you Artemis. You have this outlook on life that's just amazing and positive. You know me, always the timid shy one, but you, you are so strong and outstanding of a person, you're outgoing and strong willed and hardheaded. Those are all the qualities I admire about you and look up to. I do love and care about you, Artemis." Cassia breathed a sigh of relief, it felt good to get that off her chest. Still, Cassia felt the sting of tears welling up in her eyes.

"Aww Cass, come here" Artemis said, opening up her arms for a hug. "I've got to get going, I have to prepare for school in the morning, but we'll talk later okay, how about tomorrow after school, I can tell you all about it." Artemis said while hugging Cassia.

"Okay, sounds good" Cassia said, still in Artemis's embrace. Artemis finally let go and walked to the door, "see you later, love you."

"Love you too", Cassia felt a twinge of pain in her chest.

As Artemis was leaving, she ran into two of the Shield units, except they didn't stop her this time, but they seemed to be walking in the direction of Cassia's house.

"Hmm, I wonder if they're going to visit Cass and give her more information on her parents and sister." Artemis wondered to herself, "I'll have to ask her about that."

Artemis continued her walk home. She had made it home just in time when it started to rain again, the flesh burning acid rain that was common this time of year. When the Consortium started creating the AI, they had these huge factories that let off all kinds of chemicals and gasses, it was during the 'Happening' that the skies changed as did the weather, thus creating the acid rain they had been dealing with. According to the AI scientists, the weather patterns and acid rain specifically shouldn't last too much longer, only a couple more years. Only a couple.

"Mom, dad? I'm home." Artemis said.

"Oh sweety, thank goodness, we were so worried about you with the rain coming and all. How is Cassia doing?" Gwenvere said.

"I'm okay mom, everything is fine, Cassia is fine"

"Is everything really fine? It doesn't seem like it" Gwenvere pressed.

"It's just a little complicated and confusing between Cass and I right now, that's all, but we'll work through it. I have to get prepared for school tomorrow."

"Oh that's right, that starts tomorrow" Dnaru said, "you'll be fine sweety."

"I know dad, thanks", Artemis said and walked to her room. In her room she grabbed her backpack and started packing it with what she might need tomorrow at school. She packed her notebooks and pencils, some snacks and her data pad. She then got ready for bed, took a shower, brushed her teeth and got in her pajamas, then hopped into bed. She sunk down into the bed and pulled the covers up to her nose. The weight of everything the past few weeks had been weighing her down and she hadn't realized. Artemis lay in bed staring up at the ceiling. In that moment, she wanted to message Talin and talk with him. She needed a friend who wasn't Cassia, who wasn't involved with her in any sort of way other than just being friends. Instead,

Artemis just rolled on her side and closed her eyes, sleep would come easy to her tired weary soul.

The next morning Artemis woke up, eager to start the day. She got up, brushed her teeth and got dressed in her usual clothing of black skinny cargo pants, a light gray hooded sweatshirt, a dark grey jacket over it, and some black boots. Her hair was thrown up in the usual high ponytail with her bangs hanging down in her face. She slung her backpack over her shoulder and headed out to the kitchen. There in the kitchen stood Gwenvere with a tear in her eye. "Hey mom" Artemis said, as she grabbed the usual stuff to make her porridge and fruit.

"Oh, hey sweety, ready for your big day?" Gwenvere said with a sniffle.

"Mom, are you crying? What's wrong?"

"Oh it's nothing sweety, it's just that, you're so grown. You're such a fine young woman and now you're taking on this new adventure. You're so courageous and spirited. I still remember the day you came into this world. You've always been such a fighter. I'm just so proud of you sweety"

"Oh mom, I love you" Artemis said walking over and hugging Gwenvere, finishing up her oatmeal.

"Now, you should probably get going, you don't want to be late." Gwenvere said, and Artemis walked out of the house towards the train station. When she got to the train station, Artemis started feeling the butterflies in her stomach that she had been telling Talin about. She was both nervous and excited. She only had to wait ten minutes for the train to come. Once on board the train, she messaged Talin: *"Hey Talin, how are things?"*

"Hey Artemis, things are good. How are things with you?"

"Not too bad, I'm on the train into the city now for my first day of school"

"Oh that is exciting. Are you nervous or excited?"

"I'm both actually" Artemis responded.

"Well, I am sure you'll do great. Do you know your schedule yet? If you have any breaks, we could meet at the café?"

"That would be nice. I don't know my schedule yet but when I figure it out, I'll let you know."
The train slowed as it pulled into the station, Artemis was feeling the butterflies even stronger now, but she was ready. It was for the Defiance after all. Artemis hopped off the train and headed towards the direction of the school. Once there, she went inside and went to the reception desk.

"Hello, my name is Artemis Xeron and I'm here for my first day of school"

"Hello Artemis, and welcome to the Stellar Institute of Technology and Design, here is a schedule of your classes and labs, you don't want to be late, so I suggest you take some time to figure out where all your classes are."

"Thank you. Where is this first class?"

"You can find AI tech and design on level 4 in room 402 which will be to the right when you get off the elevator."

"Okay, thank you." Artemis looked over her schedule, she had a break after her first two classes so she messaged Talin to let him know when she would be free. *"Hey Talin, I just received my schedule, it looks like I have a free period after my first two classes, so we can meet up for coffee then."*

"Sounds good, see you then". Artemis then headed up to her first class. She walked into the classroom and took a seat, she hoped there wasn't assigned seating, but the professor wasn't there yet so she couldn't ask. There were a few other students already in the classroom in their seats, it looked like it was all Uppers, she was the only human. Most of the professors were also all AI, there were only a few of them that were human, which Artemis was surprised

to learn that the Stellar Consortium let humans teach at their school.

"Good morning class", said a smartly dressed AI as he walked into the classroom. The thing that stood out about this Upper was that he wore glasses. The AI didn't need to wear glasses, as they had perfect eyesight, and if there was a problem with their eyesight then they would just get their eyes fixed. Artemis assumed this professor wore them to give him that scholarly look. The professor continued on about expectations for the class, the syllabus, and what they would be learning today. Class was quite interesting for Artemis, she got to learn more about AI and their technology that makes them up and how they were designed. Artemis had a new understanding and appreciation for the Uppers, but she still didn't fully trust or like them. Class seemed to go by pretty fast according to Artemis.

When class was dismissed, and she headed towards her next class, she was surprised at the time already. Her next class was a government class that was all about the Stellar Consortium. Artemis was not looking forward to this class as she knew it would be all propaganda about the government and how they're so great and did so many amazing things for the city. It took all of Artemis' willpower to not constantly roll her eyes and scoff during class. This class had a few other humans in it. Artemis was glad to know she wasn't alone, but she wasn't sure where the classmates' loyalties lay; if they supported the government or not. She couldn't get a good read of them during class. Artemis was thankful once the class was done. She now had her break, so she messaged Talin that she was on her way to the café. Artemis walked to the café and was stopped by the Shield units.

"Name?"

"Xeron, Artemis Xeron, yes I'm on the list, I know. I'm just heading towards the café as I'm on break right now from the SITD and I'm meeting a friend, Talin", Artemis said already knowing everything they were going to ask her.

"Talin Viltri?"

"Yes, I believe he's also a shield unit"

"Yes, he is. Okay, you are free to go."

"Well, that was easier than normal" Artemis thought to herself and continued walking to the café. "I wonder if there will be a time when they don't actually stop me, they never do anything, just ask me the basic questions. I never am doing anything they actually care about that they know of."

Artemis reached the café and went inside, this time ordering a regular hyperbrew latte as she was feeling a little tired. She also ordered a sandwich as she decided she would use this as her lunch time. Artemis went and grabbed an open seat and waited for Talin to show up. After about ten minutes of waiting, Talin still hadn't showed up, when Artemis' data pad went off, she looked and had a message from Talin. *"Hey Artemis, I got called in for something with the Shield so I will not be able to make our lunch date, can we reschedule?"*, the message said. "Date?" Artemis questioned out loud, then responded, *"hey sure that's okay, no problem. I'll let you know when my next break is another day, and we can meet up."* Artemis found herself mildly disappointed that she wouldn't see Talin, she was looking forward to having a conversation with him, especially after her class of AI tech and design. Artemis finished up her lunch and headed back to the school for her afternoon classes. The rest of the day went by relatively fast for her and before she knew it, she was on the train headed back home.

Artemis arrived home and told her parents all about her day at school, things she learned and what she did. She was looking forward to her next day of school where she would have a lab class.

"So anyway, that was my day at school. I had a break in between classes, and I was supposed to meet my friend Talin, but he got held up with something else, so we had to reschedule"

"Talin is your AI friend, right?" Dnaru asked

"Yes, dad, he's an Upper and in the Stellar Shield"

"Is he handsome?" Gwenvere asked

"Mom" Artemis whined, "stop. Yes, he's handsome, but I have Cassia. He and I are just friends."

"Okay sweety I was just asking. Speaking of Cassia how is she doing?"

"She's better, actually, I want to talk to her and let her know how my day went, I know she's waiting for that." Artemis said.

Artemis then walked into her room and pulled out her data pad, messaging Cassia. *"Hey Cass, how are you doing? I had my first day of school today and it went well, I just wanted to tell you about it."*

"Hey Artemis, I'm doing much better thanks, and that's great to hear, I'm glad you had a good day. Did you learn anything interesting?"

"Yes, I found my AI tech and design course very interesting and learned a lot there. I could do without the

government class though, it's just *Stellar Consortium propaganda.*" Artemis said.

"*Makes sense, they founded the school and it's geared mainly towards Uppers. It should help you in the Silicon Defiance though, no? Like you can tell them what they're teaching you about the Consortium.*" Cassia replied.

"*That's true, that's my main reason for going to the school in the first place, to be closer to the city and the Uppers and see what the Stellar Consortium is all about.*"

"*So when is your next school day?*" Cassia asked.

"*Tomorrow. I was supposed to meet Talin on my break today but he got caught up in something else, so we have to reschedule, so I'm going to see if he is able to meet up tomorrow during one of my breaks.*"

"*Oh, that'll be good if you can meet up with him, I still don't really get it since he's an Upper, and a Shield unit, but you do you.*"

"*I know you don't understand, and that's okay, as long as you support me is all I need*"

"*Of course, I support you in everything you do*"

"*Alright, well I'm going to go to bed, I have an early day tomorrow. Love you Cass*"

"*Love you Artemis, talk later.*"

Artemis set her data pad in her backpack and climbed into bed. There she let the weight of the day roll off her shoulders and she sunk low into the bed, pulled the covers up to her chin, and closed her eyes. She was fast asleep.

*****

Talin had been looking forward to meeting up with Artemis on her lunch break from school. He couldn't wait to see her again and talk with her. He found her fascinating, unlike any of the other humans he had encountered. She was quick-witted and funny, not to mention beautiful. But Artemis had Cassia. If Talin wanted to be a downright prick, he could make Cassia go away by pulling some strings, but he wouldn't do that, it would hurt Artemis too much and he didn't want her to be hurt. As an AI, he initially had the emotion of sadness and remembered that he hated the sensation it caused, so he wouldn't want to inflict that on anybody.

It was the day Talin was supposed to meet Artemis, when Talin got a call from Xarius, or lead 124. They wanted him to come in to discuss something very important about his being on the Shield. He wasn't sure what it could be, as most of his job had been routine; there was nothing crazy he had to do yet, not even dispatching a human. He figured it would have to do with his request to not go through with programming. Somehow, they let him continue on with work without having been reprogrammed but said they would revisit it at a later date, Talin assumed this was the later date.

Talin took out his data pad and messaged Artemis that he wouldn't be able to make it and asked if they could reschedule. To his delight, she said yes, that wasn't a problem. Talin then headed for the Shield headquarters where his meeting was to be held. Talin walked in and walked to the employee elevator and swiped his badge, the elevator dinged and opened, and he stepped in, scanning the buttons for number four. In a flash, the elevator shot up and he was on floor number four. He exited the elevator and looked around for lead 124, or Xarius. He finally made eye contact with him and walked over.

"Hey Xarius"

"That is lead 124 to you. This is work business, you are here as an employee, not a friend, so please, use my work identifier." Lead 124 said.

"Oh, okay, sorry, lead 124" Talin said. Xarius seemed much rougher today than his normal coarse personality. Lead 124 motioned for Talin to follow him and walked into one of the briefing rooms.

"So can you tell me what this is about?" Talin asked

"It's a couple of things. First, I know you didn't get reprogrammed but yet they somehow let you start work anyway, so that's one matter that will be discussed, but secondly, word has come around that you have a human friend." Xarius said with almost disgust.

"I didn't think it was against the law to have a human friend? I didn't see anything that said there was a prohibition on that"

"There isn't Talin, it's just that, you're a shield unit, and one who has kept their emotions instead of them being reprogrammed out of you. Because of those two things, there is a question of your objectivity. Would you be able to do what is necessary to a human if you have a human friend and have your emotions?"

"Definitely. My friendship won't get in the way of work, and I keep my emotions in check, besides I don't even have all of the emotions, and as I originally stated, I believe having my emotions is helpful in this job."

"Well, you will have to convince the board of that."

"The board?"

"Yes. The board that makes up the top of the Shield. They were handpicked by the Stellar Consortium themselves to run the Stellar Shield. Oh, and one other thing, dealing with your…friend. She often drops your name whenever she is stopped by the patrol Shield units. That's how we got word that you had this friend, because she would often say she was visiting you or talking to you. Do you know about this?"

"No, I had no idea she kept name dropping me but I am sure she had good reason to. I will ask her about it next time I talk to her."

"I don't think you're quite getting it Talin." Xarius said taking a step towards Talin. "The board isn't happy that this human is using your name like that, and that you seem to be close to her. I wouldn't be surprised if they demanded you stop all communication with her."

"What? But she's done nothing wrong, neither have I, I don't want to end my friendship with her, just cause some board members who sit on their asses all day in their suit and ties are unhappy with how I'm living my life. No, that's not going to happen."

"Alright, well I'm just telling you what to expect. The board should be here any minute, so look sharp."

"Are you staying with me?" Talin asked

"No, I won't be allowed, the board wants to talk to you and only you." Lead 124 said, and walked to the door, "I believe in you, you'll be fine kid," and walked out, leaving Talin standing there alone. Well, at least Xarius believed in Talin and figured he would be fine. Was Talin's thermal processing unit broken or was it extra cold in the room? Talin was feeling nervous, if there was a word for him to put towards how he was feeling. Oh how he wanted to message Artemis, that was probably the last thing he needed to do at this moment, based on the meeting he was about to have.

Soon, five Uppers walked into the room, all dressed in business suits. Each had a serious unamused look on their faces. They each took a seat around the table and motioned for Talin to have a seat. Talin took his seat and waited for one of them to speak.

"Talin Viltri is it?"

"Yes, sir." Talin said, looking into the AI's cold dead eyes.

"Do you know why you are here today?"

"I have an idea"

"Why don't you tell us about your refusal to be reprogrammed when you knew it was part of the job. You should have been made well aware of that part when you applied for the job."

"Well, it was not so much refusal as I suggested I don't go through with reprogramming, and they agreed with me as to why I should not go through with it. That's all."

"Go ahead and tell us why you shouldn't go through with it." Another of the AI asked in a grating robotic voice.

"Well, you see, we deal with humans a lot, that's the main duty of ours, to keep the humans, especially the cogs, in line. And humans, they are emotional creatures, their emotions guide them and often led them in their actions and conversations. As one who also has feelings and emotions, I can better understand where the humans are coming from, and I can even, what's the word, empathize, with them in their situation."

"Do you not feel that makes you weaker? Does that not mean that you wouldn't be able to do what was necessary with your feelings?"

"No, I do not think so. For example, humans used to have these creatures they kept as 'pets'. Sometimes the pets got really sick and so the humans would pay for a pet doctor to kill the animal. It was seen as the humane thing to do to put the animal out of its suffering. The human doctor, being human, had emotions and feelings, but they were still able to do what was necessary. I view this job the same way."

"Ah so the humans are like animals in your view," one AI asked while a few of the AI murmured.

"Sure, I guess so" Talin said and shrugged. He didn't want to say the truth, that he thought they were more than animals, I mean look at Artemis, she was a perfect human, not some animal to be discarded away, but he couldn't tell the board that.

"Very well. We will take your viewpoints into consideration when we discuss this. Now, what can you tell us about this human you have a relationship with, this Artemis Xeron?"

Talin felt himself stiffen ever so slightly. "What about Artemis Xeron?"

"Tell us your relationship with her, tell us about her, what do you know of her?"

"Well, we are just friends. We just recently started talking and hanging out. I know she is incredibly smart, funny, and quick-witted, very different from the other humans I have encountered."

"Do you actually know anything of her or her family? Do you know she is on the Shield's watch list?" one of the AI asked pointedly.

"I was made aware she was on the list, but I'm not really sure why"

"Let's just say she is one for us to watch. We've gotten information that she may be involved with the Silicon Defiance. Have you heard of that group?"

"Yes, I've heard of them. They are an anti-Consortium group. You think Artemis is involved with them?"

"We have reason to believe she is, yes. She is aware she is on the list; the curious thing is she drops your name whenever she is stopped. Do you think she is using her connection to you in an attempt to throw us off her?"

"I highly doubt that. I don't think she has anything to hide. How long has she been on this list, and have you found anything yet that links her to the Defiance?"

"She has been on the list for a while, and no, as of right now we don't have any concrete proof linking her to the Defiance, we just have word of mouth from another human about her actions."

"Someone is telling on Artemis?" Talin asked, surprised.

"Do you know who it might be?"

"No, I have no idea. I have no other information about Artemis."

"Okay, well it is our recommendation that you cease all communication with this Artemis girl. It would be in your best interest. It doesn't look good for you to be talking with and hanging with a human who is on our watch list for potential Defiance activity."

"Is that an order? Besides, would you not want me to get closer to her? She might slip up and tell me something that is good for the Shield to know."

"Ah, that is not something we had considered", the five board members sat pondering. They then huddled together to discuss. They then turned back to Talin. "You raise a good point, if you can get close enough to her, she might slip up and tell you what she's actually doing, if she's a part of the defiance. We will use you to spy on her, and you can report her actions back to us."

"I can do that" Talin said, although he hated the idea of spying on Artemis. He didn't want to report on her actions and their conversations, but this was a better alternative to not being able to speak or hang out with her at all. Besides, he was curious about her, and if she really was a member of the Defiance. The meeting finished, and the board members took their leave, leaving Talin standing in the briefing room alone, he wanted to message Artemis, but he thought it probably wasn't a good idea to do so at that moment.

Chapter 9

It was the next morning, and Artemis woke up as usual and did her normal morning routine. Get up, get dressed, brush her teeth, go into the kitchen for breakfast, her usual of porridge. She was looking forward to school today, specifically her lab classes and her break time to meet up with Talin. Artemis said goodbye to her mom, her dad was still sleeping, and she headed off towards the train station. At the train station, it was full of people headed towards the fields. There were only a few other humans waiting for the train into the city. The train arrived after about ten minutes. Artemis hopped on board and grabbed her seat and settled in for the thirty-minute journey.

The train arrived at the station and Artemis hurried up towards the school so she wouldn't be late. As soon as Artemis got to school, she looked up her schedule and noticed when her breaks were, and messaged Talin while walking to her class. She wasn't paying attention to where she was going when she ran into an Upper who was walking the opposite direction.

"Hey, watch where you're going, filthy human, who even let you into this school?"

"Listen circuit for brains, I got a scholarship into this school thank you very much, so I probably deserve to be here more than you, next time, why don't you watch where you're going." Artemis shot back.

"I will call the Shield on you, then what'll you do?"

"Go ahead, see if I care, you'll just make me late for class is all."

"We'll see about that; I'll tell the director of the school and get you kicked out."

"I highly doubt that will happen, but you can sure try." Artemis said while the Upper grabbed his data pad and dialed in for the Shield. Artemis couldn't have looked more annoyed if she tried, but she stayed put and waited for the Shield to arrive.

Soon, three Shield members walked up to them and Artemis couldn't believe her eyes. There he was, Talin Viltri, doing his job.

"What seems to be the problem here?" Talin asked the other Upper who had called.

"This *human* ran right into me and then gave me attitude about it. I want her kicked out of the school." The Upper said. Talin then turned to see this *human* and was both surprised and not surprised to find it was Artemis Xeron.

"Hey Talin" Artemis said, shooting a glance over at the Upper who called the Shield on her.

"Hello, Ms. Xeron, care to explain what happened here?" Talin asked.

"Sure, I was walking and messaging you at the same time, and I didn't see this Upper walking towards me, and we collided. That's all."

"And what about you being rude to him?"

"Well, he was rude first, so I just gave it back."

"I see", Talin said while laughing internally. This was the Artemis he knew. "So was this just an accident then?"

"Yes" Artemis said.

"Very well, listen, sir, it seems to have just been an accident, and apparently you weren't very nice about it to begin with, so how about we just go our separate ways for the day huh?"

"But but" the Upper said stammering, "No! I want her kicked out of the school!"

"Well, we're not going to do that over an accident. If you have any further problems, you can take it up with the schools' director. We'll write up a report of the incident that transpired and you both will receive a copy as well as the school." Talin motioned to one of the other Shield units to write up the report. "Now, if there's nothing else, we will be leaving now, try to stay out of trouble you two" Talin said with a wink towards Artemis. Soon after, a ding emitted from Artemis' and the Upper's data pad, they had received the report the Shield unit wrote up.

"This is not fair. Stay out of my way human, you understand?" the Upper said, and continued on his way. Artemis just smirked at him and walked to her class. She was now late because of the incident, but hopefully the professor would understand. Artemis walked into the class and took the closest seat she could find.

"Nice of you to join us Ms. Xeron" the professor said.

"I'm sorry professor, I had an incident that involved the Shield being called. Everything is okay now though."

"Well glad you could make it. Hopefully one of your classmates can fill you in on what you missed. Now, where was I?" the professor continued. Class went by quickly, as Artemis missed half of it anyway, and she was headed towards her next class. She had a break after so she took out her data pad; *"Hey Talin, I have a break coming up, would you like to meet up for coffee?"* the message said. Talin responded, *"Sure, just let me know what time and I'll be there."* Artemis attended her next class which dragged on according to her, so she was glad when it was finally over, and she had a break. Artemis headed over to the coffee shop and waited for Talin to show up. A few minutes later, Talin walked in the door.

"Hey Artemis! I am sorry I had to cancel last time, let me buy your drink to make it up to you."

"Oh well thank you Talin, that's very kind of you."

"What would you like?"

"I'll take a hot Sitarine tea and a biscuit."

"Okay, I will be right back." Talin said as he walked over to the ordering screen. After a couple of minutes, he walked back over to where Artemis was sitting and handed her the drink and food. Talin, being AI, didn't order anything for himself.

"So, how has school been?" Talin asked, taking a seat across from Artemis.

"It's been good. Some of my classes are actually really interesting, some of them are kind of boring. I have one or two classes I could care less about but, they're part of the curriculum so I have to take them." Artemis said taking a sip of her tea, the warm slightly bitter taste causing her mouth to slightly pucker.

"Oh, which classes?"

"Well my favorite class is AI technology and design, my least favorite class is government."

"Why do you not like the government class?"

"It's just not for me. Everything they're teaching I just don't really care to learn about." Artemis had to be careful not to say her true thoughts on the class, how it was just government propaganda. Talin was curious to hear Artemis' thoughts on school, and not that he wanted to tell on her, but he was wondering if she would slip up and mention something about disliking the government and maybe being part of the Defiance. If that was the case, could Talin continue to be friends with her?

"Tell me a little about yourself, your family, I know nothing about you but consider you a friend." Talin said.

"Well, you already know my name, I'm 27 years old. I live with my mom and dad, Gwenvere and Dnaru. I'm an only child. I love my parents, they're everything to me, they've worked so hard to give me a decent life. They worked the vegetable fields, like most of the humans do, although they're retired now. I also have Cassia, whom you met. We're sort of a thing, I think, I don't really know, it's a little complicated between us. And yea, that's about it." Artemis said, taking a bite out of her biscuit. It was a little dry, so she washed it down with some tea.

"Okay, well now I feel I know you a little bit better, so that's good. As for me, I too am an only child. My parents are Lucretia and T'evse Viltri. They are high ranking executives of some business, it is rather boring, I won't bore you with the details. They however have a strong dislike of humans, and they would hate that I am hanging out with you. They also do not understand my want to be a part of Shield, they were against that as well. Oh, and I'm 31 years old, well my body is made up to be 31 years old. I have not had my adult programming for that long."

"Sounds confusing." Artemis stated, aware that Talin had just used "won't" instead of "will not", but she didn't say anything. Maybe her human-ness was rubbing off on Talin and he was warming up.

"I guess it can be if you are not used to it. Are you aware of how we grow and become adults?"

"Yes I have an idea, it's something that was sort of touched upon in class."

"So you know we start off as 'babies' with minimal programming, and after a certain time we get upgraded to a child's programming and have our neural circuit implanted into a child's body and the baby's body is reused for a new baby, and so on so forth until we reach adult programming"

"Yes, I follow" Artemis said, while having more tea and biscuit.

"They make adult bodies of different ages, and so you could have just had your adult programming yesterday but be in the body of a fifty-four year old, doesn't mean you're actually fifty-four. Technically you would only be a day-old adult, but because of the body you're in, you would say you are fifty-four. Make sense?"

"Ah okay, I'm following. So do you remember when you got your adult programming?" Artemis asked.

"Yes, I actually was not thrilled to get my adult programming, I enjoyed being a teenager, although I was glad to be able to move out of my parent's house and get my own place. It has not been that long." Talin responded. "And, unlike you, I don't really care for my parents. They are very cold AI, there is no warmth or love, like your parents give you. My parents only care about their business, and want me to follow suit, but no thank you."

"Well I'm sorry you don't have lovely parents. I don't know what I would do without mine. Which makes me feel so bad for Cassia, her parents have been gone for quite a while now, who knows when they're coming back, if they come back at all."

"What exactly happened with Cassia's parents? If you don't mind me asking, of course"

"Oh it's no problem. They were taken by the Shield along with her little sister. They were taken for reconditioning, but they haven't returned yet, although I've seen some Shield members headed towards Cassia's house a few times so I'm assuming they were giving updates on her parents. Last I know, her parents were actually doing fine, as well as her little sister who ended up not being reconditioned, but placed in an intensive class to relearn about the Stellar Consortium."

"I see, well that is unfortunate for Cassia, and I am sorry to hear the Shield did that. Do you know why?"

"I don't really want to talk about it, it'll get me riled up."

"That is understandable."

"Well, my break is almost over, I should head back to the school, I have a lab class next."

"Okay well it was nice seeing you again Artemis."

"Good seeing you too Talin. Talk later?"

"Sure" Talin said with a soft smile. Talin was looking forward to talking to Artemis again, he enjoyed their conversations. Artemis stood up and smiled at Talin, then turned and walked away. Talin could've swore his heart skipped a beat, was it a mechanical flaw he had or was that the effect Artemis had on him?

Artemis got back to the school and went to her lab class; there they were learning more about the AI bodies and how they functioned. They had a single AI in class that they were going to be working on, it was a test subject. This was good information for Artemis to learn, she could learn what makes the AI body tick, and how to power them down. This was information that she should pass on to the Defiance. Before Artemis knew it, the school day had ended, and she was on the train back home. She found herself quite tired as she had an early morning and a long day, so she fell asleep on the train. When the train arrived at the station, another human woke Artemis up.

"Excuse me miss? Is this your stop?"

"Oh yes, it is, thank you" Artemis said groggily. Artemis walked off the train and did a big yawn and stretch, now she had to walk all the way home from the train station. It was a good 20-minute walk. Luckily the weather was pleasant outside. Artemis took her time strolling home. While on her walk home, she took out her phone and messaged Cassia. *"Hey darling, I'm back from school. I had a pretty good day today. The lab class I had was very interesting, I can't wait to tell you about it. I also met up with Talin for coffee, he bought it for me to make up for missing the other day. Can't wait to see you and talk to you."*

"Hey Artemis, if you want you can come over now, I'm not doing anything."

"Thanks for the invite but I'm real tired, I think I'm going to go home and crash."

"You could always come over and spend the night with me."

"Well then, I guess I'll do that. Let me stop by my house first and pack my bag and let my parents know I'll be staying at your place tonight." Artemis said. Artemis arrived home and walked inside. "Hi mom, dad I'm home from school."

"Ah Artemis dear, how are you sweety? How was your day?" Gwenvere asked. She was in the kitchen preparing dinner.

"It was good mom, thanks for asking. I had some interesting classes, especially my lab class. Anyway, I'm going to spend the night over at Cassia's tonight, is that okay?"

"Sure darling, that should be fine, isn't it Dnaru?"

"Mmhmm, I don't have a problem with it" Dnaru said.

"Thanks guys. Well, I'm just going to go pack my bag and head over. I'm so tired so I'll probably crash early."

"Just be safe my love. I love you so much."

"I love you too mom." Artemis walked over and hugged and kissed her mom. "Hey mom, dad? I just want to thank you for being amazing parents, you guys are the best and I don't know what I would do without you."

"Oh sweety, we just love you so much, thanks for being a great daughter" Dnaru said, Gwenvere had tears in her eyes. Artemis then went to her room and started packing.

"Alright guys, I'm headed out, you all be safe without me here, don't go getting into any trouble." Artemis said and walked out the door. She arrived at Cassia's and Cassia let her in.

"Hey Artemis, come on in."

"Hey Cassia" Artemis said hugging Cassia and kissing her on the head. "I am so tired. Where am I sleeping tonight?"

"Well, I've been sleeping in my parent's room on their bed since they're…not here. You can sleep in there if you want, or you can take the sofa."

"Where are your siblings going to sleep?"

"Well X'ela has been sleeping in the room with me, and Treele has taken the sofa and Astrid has taken to some blankets on the floor."

"I guess I'll sleep in the bed with you then" Artemis said as Cassia felt a flutter in her chest, she was going to sleep in the same bed as Artemis. "Well, I am so tired, I think I'm going to go lay down now. We can talk tomorrow if that's okay."

"Sure of course, right this way to the room."

Cassia led the way to the bedroom and showed Artemis where it was. Artemis quickly got changed into her night clothes and hopped into bed. It wasn't as comfortable as her bed was, and the pillow was as flat as a pancake, but Artemis didn't mind too much, she knew the Graif's didn't have money for luxuries such as nice pillows and a mattress. It didn't really matter that the pillow and mattress weren't great though, Artemis was so tired she fell right asleep. Cassia joined her not too long after. At one point, Artemis wrapped her arms around Cassia, and Cassia nestled into Artemis' arms and fell asleep.

Morning came and Artemis woke right up, with Cassia still sleeping next to her. Artemis stroked Cassia's hair and kissed her cheek, Cassia rolled over. Artemis then got up out of bed and went to the kitchen to see what food they had for breakfast. She was trying to be as quiet as possible to not wake up the other sleeping Graif siblings. To Artemis' surprise, there was porridge available, but no fruit. Fruit wasn't something Cassia could afford but that was okay. The porridge was a nice surprise, especially since Cassia didn't even like porridge; she bought it specifically for Artemis. Artemis was in the kitchen eating, when finally, Cassia came out. The other Graif siblings started to rouse as well.

"Good morning" Artemis said.

"Good morning" Cassia responded back groggily. Treele and Astrid both got up and headed towards the kitchen.

"I see you found the porridge sissy bought for you" Astrid said.

"I did, thank you so much Cass", Artemis said while giving Cass a one-handed hug around the shoulders.

"Well I just know how much you love your porridge for breakfast, so I figured I would get some to have here for you. I'm sorry there is not fruit though, I just couldn't afford that."

"Oh don't worry about, plain porridge is still delicious."

"So do you have school today?"

"No, today is a day off. Although I think there is a Silicon Defiance meeting tonight that I'm going to attend. I have some stuff to tell them, things I learned in school.

"Oh, like what kinds of things?"

"You know, stuff about the AI, how the AI work, how they're programmed, and how their kill switch is designed. I learned all of that in my AI tech and design class and lab class. It's kind of interesting that's what they're teaching us, all about AI, considering most of the students are in fact AI."

"Yea what if a member of the Silicon Defiance was in the class and used that information to take them down? *Cough cough*" Cassia said while doing a fake cough.

"Whatever." Artemis said, while rolling her eyes. "So what do you want to do today? I have a lot of time before the Defiance meeting, and my parents know I'm over your place so I should be good."

"I don't know, I hadn't really thought that far. What do you want to do?"

"We could…go into the city?"

"What is it with you and going into the city now? You never used to go into the city and now you want to go all the time. Is it Talin?"

"Why, you jealous of him?" Artemis teased.

"N – No, I'm not jealous of him, I have no reason to be, right? I just don't like the city. Too many Uppers and Shield units there.

"Babe, there's Shield units all over, even over here where we live there's constant patrols by the Shield units. And the Uppers, they're fine for the most part, if you don't bother them, they don't bother you. Oh, speaking of which, did I tell you what happened at school with an Upper? This will make you not want to go near them haha"

"No what happened?" Knowing Artemis, it was something that was probably avoidable but her big mouth got her into trouble.

"So I was walking and messaging Talin and I walked right into an Upper, of course he got all snippy with me and called me a filthy human and he wanted me kicked out of the school, and he called the Shield on me. Well, three Shield units came and guess who one of them was,

Talin Viltri. Well, they basically decided that it was accidental and there was no harm done and so they wrote up a report of the incident and sent it to me, the Upper, and the director of the school, cause the Upper wasn't happy with the outcome and was going to go to the school about getting me kicked out, but the director has a report of what happened, so, I don't think I'm getting kicked out."

"Oh Artemis" Cassia said sighing. "This is why I worry about you."

"What? I did nothing wrong."

"What did you say to him? Cause I know him calling you a filthy human did not sit well with you."

"I might have called him circuits for brains and told him maybe he should watch where he's going next time" Artemis said while Cassia started snickering.

"Oh Artemis. I figured it was something like that. Come here" Cassia said opening her arms wide, Artemis walked forward and into her arms and they embraced each other. "You know I love you right Artemis, I really do care about you, please don't ever forget that, no matter what."

"Why are you acting all weird for, of course I know you love me, who doesn't?" Artemis said grinning.

"I'm serious Artemis. Please tell me you know."

"Okay okay fine, yes, I'm aware that you love me and care about me, no matter what." Then Artemis leaned forward and planted a kiss directly on Cassia's lush ruby red lips. Cassia was slightly stunned and didn't know what to do. That was the first time they had ever kissed, and while Cassia had waited for it and wanted it to happen, she was also stunned that this was the moment that it happened in. Cassia then snapped out of it and stepped forward grabbing Artemis' face with both of her hands and kissed her back with a passion she had been saving all this time. Artemis' heart was pounding in her chest, adrenaline coursing through her body, she loved Cassia with all her might and let her know it through her kiss. They stood there for a few minutes gazing into each other's eyes, when Artemis finally spoke up and said "so, about going into the city?" and Cassia laughed.

"Way to break the tension." Cassia said.

"Nah there was no tension, but it was a little awkward just standing there staring at each other."

"Ever the romantic." Cassia teased. "Fine, we can go into the city. Are you going to try and meet up with Talin?"

"I might message him and see. In fact, let me do that now." Artemis took out her data pad, *"Hey Talin,*

Cassia and I are headed into the city, want to meet up at the café?"

"Sure, I'd love to." Talin responded. Artemis and Cassia then headed to the train station, boarded the train and headed into the city.

*****

Talin had very much enjoyed his meeting with Artemis. He enjoyed her company and their conversation. He was able to find out a little more about Artemis, but nothing crazy like if she was a member of the Silicon Defiance. Which was good because he was supposed to report on her to the board, of which he had a meeting with them today.

"Well let's hear it. Did you find anything out about the human girl, Artemis Xeron?" one of the board members asked Talin.

"Well, not much. I learned she is an only child, and she lives with her mom and dad whom she loves very much."

"Okay, good, good, we can use that. Anything else of note?"

"No, that's about it. Wait what do you mean 'we can use that'?" Talin asked, slightly concerned for his human friend.

"It's nothing that concerns you, just making a note. Now Talin, what do you know of a Cassia Graif?"

"Cassia? I don't know much about her, only she is a real close friend and girlfriend of Artemis. I know her parents and baby sister were taken to be reconditioned, and they haven't returned. That's about it. I also know she is a cog, and dislikes the Uppers and Stellar Shield."

"So Cassia and Artemis are in a relationship?"

"I believe so, although Artemis advised it was complicated."

"I see. Interesting. Well thank you for your assistance Talin, it is greatly appreciated. We look forward to more reports from you." The board members stood to get up from the table and walked out of the door. "We'll be seeing you Mr. Viltri."

"Be seeing you" Talin responded. Soon after, his data pad dinged alerting him to a message, it was from Artemis, asking him if he wanted to meet up when she and Cassia come into the city. *"Sure, I'd love to"* Talin responded. Talin was excited and couldn't wait to see Artemis again, even if she did bring along Cassia.

Chapter 10

Artemis and Cassia got to the city faster this time than normal, instead of the usual thirty minutes to get to the city, it only took them twenty minutes this time, the train had really picked up speed. Artemis and Cassia took some time to explore the city, as they had never really done so. The stayed close by to the café though so they could meet up with Talin. Maybe they could ask Talin for a tour of the city. It would be better for the two humans to have an Upper with them as they strolled around the city. Artemis and Cassia went into the café and took a seat to wait for Talin to arrive. Once Talin got there, Artemis went to order for her and Cass.

"Two Sitarine Teas and two biscuits please." Artemis ordered at the screen. The robotic machine got to work making their drinks. Soon Artemis returned to the table with the drinks and biscuits. Talin and Cassia were busy talking with each other.

"Looks like you two are getting along well," Artemis said.

"Yes, Cassia and I were having a rather pleasant conversation."

"He's actually not so bad, Artemis."

"Well good, I'm glad to hear that. So listen, Talin, we were wondering if you would give us a tour of the city, we've never actually really explored the city."

"Sure, I can do that for you. We can finish up here and head over to my place, and I'll show you different things on the way." Talin said. Artemis and Cassia finished up their drinks and eating their biscuits and they were ready to head out. Talin stood and motioned towards the door for Artemis and Cassia to walk out first. Cassia was a little hesitant to explore the city, even though Talin was with them, she didn't fully trust Talin.

"Hey, it'll be okay" Artemis said to Cassia, sensing her hesitation, "you're with me remember? Would I let anything bad happen to you?"

"No, I guess not" Cassia said.

"Of course not. You have nothing to worry about, besides we're with Talin and I trust him."

"Okay, if you say so."

"So ladies, this is Trocher city. First impressions so far?" Talin asked.

"It's big? I don't know, it's much nicer and cleaner than where the humans live, that's for sure. Everything seems shiny and new here, compared to the outer rim where we live, where everything is old and dilapidated. Rust is a common color in our parts." Cassia said.

"Yes, most of it is nice and taken care of, for the Uppers, although there are the seedy 'underground' areas that you should avoid. We won't be going to those areas, sorry to disappoint," Talin said.

"Aww bummer" Artemis joked. As they were walking through the city, Artemis grabbed Cassia's hand to help calm her down. Talin didn't know what jealousy was, but he found himself wanting to hold Artemis's hand too. They continued walking, with Talin explaining the various parts of the city to Artemis and Cass. Finally, they reached a tall building which was where Talin lived. He invited them up.

"Would you like to see where and how I live?"

"Sure, let's go" Artemis said, Cassia didn't respond. She was uncomfortable with going up into an Upper's apartment but didn't say otherwise, she would just follow

Artemis. They walked in and took the elevator to the 12th floor. Talin walked up to his door and opened it, inviting the ladies inside.

"You're not going to murder us in your apartment, are you?" Artemis asked.

"Artemis!" Cass said, sounding more nervous and panicked.

"Cass relax, I'm kidding. Obviously if I thought Talin was going to murder us I wouldn't have come up here."

Talin laughed, "no, I promise no harm will come to you while you are here with me, now let's go in." Talin walked in followed by Artemis and finally Cassia.

"Wow, look at this place." Artemis said looking around, walking up to the floor to ceiling windows that overlooked Trocher city.

Talin's apartment was very sterile and clean looking. He was also a minimalist and had very little inside his apartment, as an AI, there was very little that he actually needed. He had a one bedroom one bathroom place. In his bedroom was his recharging bed. The living room had a white sofa and a glass coffee table. The kitchen was all white with white marble counter tops.

"Talin, if AI don't eat and drink, why do you have a kitchen?"

"That's just how they were built, I think they're left over from when humans lived in the city, before they got forced to the outer rim. Besides, if we ever have humans over, we could entertain them."

"How often do AI have humans over? Don't most Uppers hate humans?"

"Well, yes, but if they didn't, then they would use their kitchens."

"Talin, may I use the restroom?" Cassia asked hesitantly.

"Of course Cassia, it is right through here," Talin said leading the way. Talin came back out and walked over to Artemis. He didn't know if he should say this, but he asked Artemis, "Artemis, has anyone ever told you how beautiful you are?"
Artemis stood there unsure of what to do or say, her cheeks tinged with slight pink.

"Uh, no, no I don't think anyone has ever told me that before." Artemis stared down and shuffled her feet around.

Compliments always made Artemis feel uneasy, she was not good at accepting them. Artemis could feel her heart beat faster and heat rush to her cheeks, she was sure she was blushing.

"C'mon Artemis, he's an Upper, and you have Cassia, pull yourself together," Artemis thought to herself. Talin could tell it made Artemis uncomfortable, so he said "listen, I didn't mean to make you uncomfortable, it was just an observation, that you are very beautiful. That's just an objective fact coming from an AI."

"I don't know how objective that is, or if it's fact. But thank you, I appreciate it." Then Cassia came back out, "What did I miss?"

"I was telling Artemis how beautiful she is, wouldn't you agree Cassia?" Cassia, unsure of Talin's intentions responded "Oh yes, 100%. Artemis is stunning, with her golden wheat hair, stunning ocean blue eyes, her strong athletic build. She's perfect."

"Oh stop it" Artemis said, now fully sure she was blushing. She really did not like compliments, they made her supremely uncomfortable. "Anyway, this is a nice place you have here."

"Thank you, I really like it a lot, I think it's a great location too."

Suddenly, Talin's door opened, and two intimidating Uppers walked in. Artemis and Cassia looked to the door and both their eyes widened.

"Oh, Talin, I didn't realize you had company over." said the male AI.

"Mom, dad? What are you doing here?" Talin asked.

"Talin, are these…humans?" Lucretia Viltri asked with a voice Artemis was sure could cut glass. The disgust in her tone was palpable.

"Mom, dad, this is Artemis Xeron and Cassia Graif, they're friends of mine, I invited them over."

"Hello" Artemis said as cordially as possible, meanwhile Cassia looked like she was about to have a stroke. Lucretia and T'evse did not have a warm inviting appearance about them, and most humans avoided crossing paths with them due to their intimidating look, so it's no wonder Cassia, who dislikes Uppers to begin with, was about the pass out at the sight of Lucretia and T'evse.

"Hello, humans" T'evse said with a tone that made the humans seem like they were vile creatures, which according to Lucretia and T'evse, the humans were.

"Talin, you know how we feel about humans, why would you bring them up to your living space? They are dirty, diseased creatures." Lucretia said with a look of disgust. The AI were not human, but boy did Lucretia master the look of distaste.

"Because mom, it is my space, and I don't mind them, as I said, they are my friends."

"Oh Talin, I will never understand." Lucretia said shaking her head. "Very well, we shall take our leave for now, we'll come by at a later time when you're not preoccupied with these filthy creatures."

"Mother." Talin scolded. Lucretia and T'evse left without another word.

"I am so sorry ladies, please excuse my parents, they're your typical Upper who dislike the humans."

"Clearly. What pleasant people." Artemis said rolling her eyes. "Cassia, you doing okay babe?" Artemis asked turning to Cassia who was white as a cloud in the sky.

"I – I'll be fine, yea, I'll be okay." Cassia said shakily, trying to steady her breath.

"Talin, I think we should probably go; poor Cassia's nerves are shot it seems like, we should get going and head for home. Thank you so much for this tour though, it was interesting and enlightening."

"Of course, anytime, I am glad to do this for you. Again, I apologize about my parents."

"It's okay, my parents aren't thrilled I have an Upper friend so, I get it. Alright, come on Cass, let's go home" Artemis said grabbing Cassia's hand and heading for the door.

"Bye Talin" Artemis said with a smile, "talk soon?"

"Of course. Goodbye."

Talin was left standing in his apartment by himself. He felt an almost sense of sadness that Artemis was gone, she had been standing in his apartment and now she was not there. That little bit of time with Artemis was enough for Talin to make him happy though, he wouldn't take that for granted.

Artemis and Cassia had a pretty silent walk to the train station, Cassia was still shaken up from Talin's parents.

"So what do you think of Talin now that you've spent some time with him, he's not bad right? Ignore his parents, of course."

"No, I guess not. I can see why you like hanging out with him. I don't have to worry about him do I, I mean you and him?"

"What? No Cass of course not, we're just friends, that's all. Besides, you saw his parent's reaction to us, I don't think it would ever work between him and I."

"Okay good, just checking. Man, his parents are scary" Cassia said letting out a laugh, Artemis joined in laughing and agreed. They got to the train station and waited about five minutes for their train to arrive. Once on board, Artemis took a nap on Cassia's shoulder. Soon, they arrived back to their hometown train station. Cassia woke Artemis up and they got off the train. They started walking in the direction of home then came to a fork in the road where Cassia goes one way and Artemis would go the other way.

"Well, looks like this is where we party ways." Cassia said.

"Yea, listen, I had so much fun with you today, thanks for coming with me" Artemis said.

"Of course, I actually enjoyed it too, except for the end there but it's fine."

"I'll talk to you later?"

"Of course. Bye." Cassia said as she started off towards her home and Artemis walked towards hers. Finally, when she got home, she shouted for her mom and dad.

"Mom? dad? I'm home!", there was no response. "Hmm weird, I didn't think they were going out anywhere. Their bedroom door is open so they're not in the room. I wonder where they could be." Artemis pondered quietly to herself. "Maybe my parents have just gone out for the evening". They rarely ever did that, but they deserved a night out. Although Artemis isn't sure where they would have gone to. Artemis pulled out her data pad to message Cassia: *"Hey Cassia, have you seen my parents by any chance on your walk home? They're not home and I'm not sure where they could be"*.

"No, I'm sorry, I haven't seen them" Cassia replied.

Artemis was tired from her day, so she went straight to her room to go to sleep. She figured her parents should return home soon so she didn't need to wait up for them. Artemis got ready for bed and went to sleep. She woke up the next morning and got dressed and walked out of her room. Her parents' bedroom door was still open from the night before, but she never heard them. Artemis first went to the bathroom to finish getting ready for the day, then walked out to the kitchen.

"Mom? Dad?" Artemis called out, but there was no response, no sign of her parents at all. "Well, maybe they came home last night and went out again today, the weather is pleasant after all." Artemis thought to herself.

She was a little nervous, but told herself to relax, that everything would be okay. She took out her data pad again, *"Hey Cass, you haven't seen my parents today yet by any chance, have you? I never saw them return last night, and today they're not here again. I assume they must've gone out again, maybe for a walk since it's nice out."* and sent the message. After a few minutes, Cass responded: *"Hey Artemis, I'm sorry but no, I haven't seen your parents. I'm sure they're just out and about and will return home soon"*. Artemis had plans for today, mainly the Defiance meeting, but she wasn't sure if she should just stay home and see when her parents return.

"No, it'll be fine, I don't have to ruin my plans. I'll just see them later when I get back. I'll make sure not to stay out too late."

Artemis went about her day doing small errands here and there like going grocery shopping at the corner store, grabbing a few needed items. Artemis had a few extra sheckles on her and so she bought her mom a nice bouquet of flowers.

"These are beautiful, I can't wait to give them to mom, she'll love them" Artemis said smiling. Artemis continued on with her day until the evening when she met up with the Silicon Defiance.

"Hey Artemis welcome back," some of the members welcomed Artemis.

"Hey guys" Artemis responded, "I have some news to share with you."

"Okay everyone settle down, we have some important news to share with you all, Artemis if you would" X'lena, the leader, said.

"So, as you all probably know, I'm a student at the Stellar Institute for Technology and Design, and two of my courses are AI technology and design classroom part and lab. In it, we're learning all about the AI, their technology, how they're built, how they "grow" or evolve, how they function, literally everything there is to know about AI we're learning it or will learn it over the course of this class."

"Well that's great, how does that help us?" a member asked.

"Because we can learn what makes them tick, and if they have an off switch, which would come in very handy for us in our attempt to take down the government, obviously" someone else replied.

"Exactly. The more we know about our 'enemy', the more prepared we will be." Artemis said.

"But isn't the Consortium our enemy, the humans? Not the Uppers?" another member said.

"Who do you think makes up the Stellar Shield? Who do you think the consortium has protecting them? It's all AI. Take out the AI and the Consortium has nothing." X'lena, said. There grew a murmuring as people started speculating and talking about the plans.

"Alright, alright, settle down now", X'lena said as a hush came over the group.

"Now, this is a long, slow process, and I know some of you might be getting frustrated with the lack of action, but listen, this is important stuff okay. It will take some time. The information Artemis is gathering for us is the most important, but it's through her classes so it's going to be the longest and slowest part. We all need to have patience, okay?" Another murmuring grew through the crowd. "That's all we have for today. You're all dismissed." X'lena said.

"Wait guys, before you leave," Artemis shouted out, "has anyone seen my parents?"

"What?" someone asked.

"My parents. Has anyone seen them? They weren't home yesterday or today when I woke up, I'm just wondering if anyone saw them out and about?"

"No, sorry" one member said.

"No" another member said.

"Nope haven't seen them."

"Alright, well thanks anyways everyone." Artemis responded.

Everyone got up and started to leave in ones and twos, as to not draw attention to themselves. Finally, Artemis said goodbye to X'lena and headed out. On her way back home from the meeting, she saw two Shield units coming back from the direction of Cassia's house.

"I wonder what they were doing there so late. But, if it's anything to do with her parents and sister, I'm sure she doesn't mind what time it is."

The two Shield units didn't see Artemis and she kept on walking. Eventually she made her way home.

"Mom? Dad? Hello?" Artemis called out, there was still no response.

The bedroom door was still open, so Artemis walked in to take a look. As soon as Artemis walked in, her heart stopped, and her stomach dropped. Blood. There was a decent amount of blood on the floor, and her parents nowhere to be found.

"Mom! Dad!" Artemis shouted as she finally started to panic. Her breathing became shallow, and the room began to spin. She turned pale. She whipped out her message pad: there was nothing from her parents. Tears started forming in her eyes, "Mom? Dad?" she cried out again. Artemis bolted out the front door and took off towards Cassia's house. When she arrived, she banged on the door until Cassia opened it looking panicked.

"What, what is it Artemis? My goodness you scared me."

"My parents!" Artemis yelled out with tears rolling down her cheeks.

"What about them Artemis? Take a deep breath and tell me what's going on?"

"Remember when I was asking you about my parents? Well, I still never saw them and when I got home today from the Defiance meeting, they still weren't home, so I went to their bedroom and there was a decent amount of blood on the floor!" Artemis said through the tears.

"Okay, Artemis, I'm sure there's a good explanation for what happened. Maybe your mom or dad hurt themselves and took themselves to the hospital and that's why you haven't seen them. You have been out and about today, right?"

"Yea I guess – wait, how do you know I've been out and about today?"

"I saw you silly. You walked by earlier, on your way home from the meeting."

"I – didn't come this far though?"

"You're always out and about, running errands or going to your Defiance meetings, or even the city nowadays. Let's focus on your parents. Did you try messaging them or calling them?"

"No…"

"Well give that a try first before you continue to freak out." Cassia said as Artemis took out her data pad and proceeded to message her mom and dad. *"Hey mom, dad, just wondering where you are since I haven't seen you, let me know you're okay"*, Artemis sent it.

"Now, try calling the hospital to see if they're there" Cassia said.

"Good idea." Artemis dialed the hospital's number, a holograph receptionist appeared.

"Please state your emergency or please hold." The hologram said, then disappeared while the Stellar

Consortium symbol appeared and hold music started to play. A few minutes went by when the hologram reappeared, "Please state your inquiry or request"

"Is there a Mr. or Mrs. Xeron there?"

"No, I am not seeing any patients with that name."

"Is there a Gwenvere or Dnaru there?"

"No, I am not seeing any patients with that name." The hologram said. Artemis hung up the call.

"Cassia" Artemis whined, "what do I do? Where are my parents?"

"I'm not sure Artemis, I'm sure they're okay though. Why don't you go home and get some rest and we'll figure this out in the morning, we can search for them."

"Can I sleep here for the night?" Artemis asked.

"Um…sure, that should be fine." Cassia said slightly hesitantly. Artemis went to the bedroom and crawled into bed, silently weeping out of fear and concern for her parents. Her poor mother was such a sweet, kind, and docile lady. Artemis couldn't bear to think about something bad happening to her. And her father, he appeared tough as nails but had a heart of gold. Dnaru was a family man, and would never let anything happen to Gwenvere, the love of his life. He would rather die than something happen to his family. Artemis continued to gently sob. Cassia came in and sat on the bed, stroking Artemis's hair. "There, there. I'm sure it will all work out. If it helps any, I know what it's like to have your parents missing." A sudden fear washed over Artemis.

"What did you say?" Artemis asked.

"That I know what it's like to have parents missing."

"But you know where your parents are, I mean they're still gone which sucks, but you know they're alive and well, right, isn't that why I always see Shield Units leaving your house, cause they're delivering news of your parents?"

"Um yea, that's true. I'm sorry, I just thought it would be helpful to know that I know what it's like to not have parents around." Cassia responded. Artemis couldn't help but fear the worst now, what if her parents were taken by Shield?

"Cass. What if my parents were taken by Shield?"

"Could be, but I'm sure you would've heard about that by now though, wouldn't you have? Did you ask Talin?"

"No, I should message him."

"Why don't you get some sleep right now, it's late okay? You can message him tomorrow, one night isn't going to change anything."

"Okay, you're right." Artemis took a deep breath. "Goodnight Cass."

"Goodnight Artemis." Cassia said as she kissed Artemis's cheek and wiped the tears from Artemis' eyes. Cassia then walked out of the door, leaving it slightly ajar. Artemis laid down and softly cried herself to sleep. It was the middle of the night when Artemis heard what sounded like fierce whispering.

"Cass?" Artemis quietly asked while feeling around in the bed. She didn't feel Cassia there. Artemis groggily got up and walked to the door and put her ear towards the opening.

"What did…and the… Shield units do?" Artemis could hear someone asking.

"We did what…to. It wasn't…choice" someone else said.

"So you…her parents. …fucks sake…you could possibly do." Artemis wasn't sure what she was hearing exactly, as she was still half asleep and they, whoever they were, were whispering. Was that Cassia talking? And to whom was she talking to? Artemis was so tired that she went back to the bed and immediately fell back asleep. When she woke up in the morning, she felt like she had the strangest dream last night. Did she dream Cassia was having a stern conversation with someone? Artemis felt over next to her and found Cass, sound asleep there. No, that couldn't have been her up talking last night, could it have been? Artemis got up out of bed and headed to the kitchen. She didn't have much of an appetite, but she made herself eat anyway. Porridge and fruit. Cassia had bought fruit, which was very rare considering their money situation, so that was sweet of Cassia. Cassia knew Artemis's breakfast of porridge wasn't complete without the fruit.

"I'll have to thank her when she wakes up." Artemis said to herself. Artemis didn't want to wait around for Cassia to wake up, she wanted to head home already in hopes that her parents would be there. Luckily, Cassia started to rouse right away.

"Hey early bird" Cass said rubbing her eyes as she walked into the kitchen. She walked over to Artemis and gave her a hug.

"Morning sleepy head." Artemis responded. "Thank you for buying some fruit for my porridge, I know money is tight for you, so I really appreciate it."

"You're welcome. So, what's the plan for today?"

"I think I'm going to go home, hopefully my parents will be there. If not, I'm going into the city to Shield headquarters and file a missing persons report, or see if they know what happened to my parents."

"Okay, do you want me to come with you?"

"No, I'll be okay, I think I'm actually going to message Talin"

"Alright, well I hope you find them." Cassia said as Artemis headed out the door. Artemis then took out her data pad and messaged Talin.

"Hey, Talin, I don't suppose you have seen or heard anything about my parents have you? I haven't seen them since the other day, and I found blood in the house and I don't know where they are or what they're up to. Please let me know."

"Hey Artemis, I am sorry to hear that, no I don't think I've heard anything about your parents, or seen them, but I can look into it if you'd like, what are their names again?"

"Gwenvere and Dnaru Xeron, but that's okay, actually, I'm going into the city to Shield headquarters to inquire about them, would you mind coming with me?"

Artemis asked, and there was a few minutes time lapse before a response came through.

"I can do that." Talin responded.

"Thank you. I'll let you know when I'm on the train into the city, it'll be about a thirty-minute trip." Artemis said and finally made it to her house. She took a deep breath, then opened the door. There still was no sign of her mom and dad. A wave of fear and panic washed over her.

"No Artemis. Be strong. Now is not the time to freak out. Figure this out first, find the rational explanation, then, you can freak out."
Artemis packed her bag and headed towards the train station. Once onboard, she messaged Talin, then settled in for the ride, trying to remain as calm as possible. The thirty-minutes felt like forever to Artemis.

*****

Talin would say he was enjoying his job as a Shield unit. Most of the time it was doing random patrols through various neighborhoods, and on occasion he got a city assignment. He felt lucky that he hadn't encountered anything crazy on his shifts so far, and he felt most lucky he didn't have to *dispatch* a human. He wasn't sure at this point if he'd even be able to do such a thing, between his emotions he had that weren't reprogrammed out of him, and Artemis, his human friend whom he found himself caring for an awful lot. It was like humans and their pets, he thought.

Talin had arrived to work when there was a commotion going on.

"What's going on? What's all the commotion about?" Talin asked.

"You didn't hear? There were two humans that were dispatched."

"Oh really, two of them, at the same time?" Talin asked, an uneasy feeling rising in his gut, he didn't like this feeling.

"Yes, well, not exactly at the same time, but one right after the other. It's very rare for two humans to be dispatched at once."

"Weren't there two others who were killed recently though?"

"Dispatched. And yes, that's why this is so crazy. It's so rare for this to happen."

"Do we know who they were?" Talin asked.

"Just some humans, apparently they have someone in the family who is in the Silicon Defiance though."

"Oh, well then why not dispatch that person, were the parents part of the defiance?"

"No, they weren't, but I guess it was a way of ensuring they don't join, and as a way to get back at the person for their activities."

"I see" Talin replied. He scouted out lead 124 and went to ask him some questions.

"Hey, lead 124, do you have any information on what's going on? I just know two humans were dispatched and that's it."

"Well, that's all you need to know. There's nothing more to it really. Just another day doing our job, and something I authorized to be done. Feeling lucky it wasn't you who had to do it?"

"I guess so." Talin said, who was in fact very relieved it wasn't his job, yet. Talin continued about his day, trying not to put too much focus on the fact that the Shield just killed two more people. Maybe this job wasn't right for Talin after all. What if it was Artemis who was part of Silicon Defiance? Would Talin be able to kill her if ordered to do so by lead 124? He probably wouldn't be able to, definitely not with his emotions still in place. Not when he found himself caring for the human. Talin's parents should be happy and proud that he was a part of

Shield, they should like the fact that they deal with humans and dispatch them when needed, considering their hate against the humans.

A few days later, Talin had received a message from Artemis, it was about her parents. Talin had not seen or heard anything about her parents unfortunately, he wanted to help her out as best as he could. He could ask at work about them, but Artemis said she's coming into the city to find out herself. She asked Talin if he could join her. That made Talin extremely happy. She wanted him to be with her.

"Just let me know when you get close, I'll meet you at the train station." Talin messaged.

Chapter 11

The train had about ten minutes left on the journey into the city, so Artemis messaged Talin.

"Hey, I'm about ten minutes away."

"Okay, I'll be there at the station waiting for you." Talin replied.

Soon, the train slowed to a roll and finally came to a complete stop. Outside the window, Artemis could see Talin standing there, handsome as always.

"Hey Talin" Artemis said stepping off the train, her eyes were red and puffy from crying.

"Hello Artemis" Talin responded. Talin felt something seeing Artemis that way.

"Ready to go to Shield headquarters?" Artemis asked.

"Ready when you are. I'm sorry about your parents, by the way." Talin said.

"What are you sorry for? You didn't do anything, right?" Artemis asked hoping the answer was no, after all, he was a Shield unit, maybe he did have something to do with her parents' disappearance.

"I promise, I had nothing to do with your parents going missing. I promise on all that I have. I haven't heard anything about a Gwenvere or Dnaru Xeron, I've been keeping my ears open."

"Okay, just had to ask. Let's go." Artemis and Talin headed off towards the Shield headquarters. They got a few stares as they walked together, but Talin figured most of the Uppers just thought it was another Shield unit escorting a human, which happened time to time. Even when he got to work, most of the Uppers would think he was the one bringing the human in. After about a ten-minute walk, they got to the Shield headquarters. Artemis stopped outside the building and took a few deep breaths.

"Are you okay?" Talin asked.

"I'm just…nervous, is all. I'm afraid of what I might find out, or not find out."

"I'm sure everything will be okay. Let's go in and see. You can hold my hand if you'd like?" Talin asked, hoping Artemis would say yes, despite the looks he would earn for holding a human's hand.

"No, I'm okay thank you. I have to be strong, for mama and papa. I'm going to walk in there, and demand answers. You can accompany me but stand back."

"Very well. Whatever you wish." Talin said as Artemis headed up the stairs and into the building. Artemis got inside and marched right up to the reception desk. The receptionist barely glanced up and asked, "how can I help you?"

"I'd like to know if there are any reports involving my parents?"

"What are their names?"

"Gwenvere and Dnaru Xeron"

"One moment please while I check the records system." A minute or so passed when finally, "There is one file I found on Gwenvere and Dnaru Xeron. Ah, it says it's a special file, may I ask who you are in relation to them?"

"I am Artemis Xeron, their daughter." The receptionist finally looked up at the human standing in front of her. "Artemis? Artemis Xeron?"

"Yes" Artemis answered.

"One moment please." The receptionist said and then glanced back at Talin. "Are you with her?"

"Yes, I accompanied her here" Talin replied.

"Very well. One moment please." The receptionist then sent a message. Soon, lead 124 came down, Talin was feeling a little nervous now.

"Artemis Xeron, is it?" Lead 124 asked, "and Talin, why am I not surprised to see you accompanied a human down here?"

"She's actually my friend Xarius" Talin said.

"Again, not surprised really, you and those emotions of yours. Anyway, Ms. Xeron, what can I do for you?"

"What do you know about my parents, Gwenvere and Dnaru Xeron? There's a special file the receptionist pulled up, but she didn't tell me what the file says, she called you instead."

"Ah, your parents are Gwenvere and Dnaru Xeron? I had no idea. Very well, follow me if you would please. Talin, you can stay behind, this doesn't concern you." Lead 124 said. Talin was feeling more nervous now, he wanted to be there for Artemis.

"Now Artemis, please, have a seat. I have some questions for you." Lead 124 said, motioning to a chair. Artemis hesitantly took a seat then said "No, tell me about my parents."

"Artemis, I'm trying to make this easy on you, it'll go much better if you cooperate."

"Fine. What do you want to know?"

"Well, first and foremost, and please be honest with me, are you a member of the rebellion group known as the Silicon Defiance?"

"What? What is this an interrogation? I'm here to find out about my parents."

"Please Artemis, just answer the question." If AI had patience, Xarius was quickly losing it with Artemis.

"No. I am not a member of Silicon Defiance" Artemis said staring straight into lead 124's eyes. He narrowed his, an artificial light shining through them, and squinted at Artemis.

"Artemis, dear, you don't want to lie to me you know."

"I know, I know, you have special lie detection abilities blah blah blah, that's what the Shield units said when they came to our house asking the same questions. Do you have anything new cause I don't."

"You are a feisty one, aren't you? No wonder Talin likes you." Artemis could feel herself slightly blush. "Fine, nothing new. Now about your parents…"

"Yes, what about them, where are they?"

"Artemis, your parents have been taken for reconditioning. It's as simple as that. We believe there is seditionary activities going on in your household and we believe reconditioning your parents was the best option."

"What?" Artemis couldn't believe what she was hearing. "My parents have nothing to do with the Silicon Defiance! They are completely innocent!"

"Are you?" Lead 124 asked.

"Am I what?"

"Completely innocent?"

"Yes, yes I am" Artemis replied.

"Well, we still believe this is the best course of action. Do not worry, your parents won't be harmed really, just reconditioned, they should still remember who you are."

"Did Talin know?" Artemis asked, afraid of what the answer might be.

"Of course, he helped take them in" Lead 124 said with an icy grin on his face. Artemis felt an icy chill run through her veins. She couldn't believe it, didn't want to believe it. Talin, the AI whom she considered a friend, had helped in taking her parents. Apparently, they did not go easily based on the blood on their bedroom floor. Artemis stood up and said, "we're done here" and stormed out of the room. She stormed all the way down to where Talin was standing and yelled at him from across the room when she saw him, "how could you?!", Talin looked taken aback.

"I'm sorry? How could I what?" Talin asked, confused.

"You knew about my parents this whole time and didn't tell me?" Artemis was still yelling but now she was standing face to face with Talin, tears stinging her eyes.

"Artemis please I have no idea what you are talking about, why don't you lower your voice some, they're all staring."

"Oh please, you know very well you helped kidnap my parents, probably injuring them when they wouldn't go willingly, just so they can be reconditioned. Lead 124 said so! And I don't care that they are staring, let them stare!"

"Lead 124? Reconditioned? Artemis please, I swear I don't know what you're talking about." Talin looked up to see lead 124 grinning at him from the top of the stairs. "Artemis, he's lying to you, I don't know why, probably because he doesn't want me being friends with you."

"Well yea, you can forget about our friendship now. I can't believe you would do this to me. Don't ever talk to me again. You betrayed me." Artemis yelled and stormed out of the building.

"Artemis wait!" Talin yelled after her, but she was already gone. "Xarius, what did you do?"

"You need to be careful with that girl. She's a part of the Defiance, you know?" Xarius said.

"Did she tell you that?" Talin asked.

"Well no, but we all know she's lying. Now with her parents gone, maybe she'll be more likely to fess up."

"Her parents…wait a minute…you didn't…Xarius, those two people you dispatched earlier, who were they?"

"Nothing for you to worry about Talin"

"Xarius, you told Artemis her parents were reconditioned."

"And that's all she needs to know, for now." Lead 124 said. Talin felt sick to his stomach, if he could even feel that way, being circuitry and all. Whatever feeling or emotion that was, he hated it. Talin then left the building. How could he continue with his job as a Shield unit knowing they lied to Artemis and turned her against him? Talin hated that Artemis hated him now, he couldn't bear to stand her being so mad at him. Talin took out his data pad to message Artemis: *"Artemis please listen to me, I swear I had no idea about your parents at all. I had nothing to do with their disappearance or their reconditioning. In fact, I*

think it's more than reconditioning, please just talk to me."
There was no response.

Artemis made it back to the train station and was still fuming. She needed to see Cassia immediately. Artemis felt her data pad go off and looked at it, it was the message from Talin. She ignored it and put her data pad back in her bag. The train eventually made it back to the outer rim of Trocher, and Artemis walked straight to Cassia's house. Artemis banged on the door when the younger Astrid answered.

"Hi Artemis!" Astrid said.

"Astrid where's Cassia? I need to talk to her."

"Oh, well she's not here right now, but she should be back soon if you want to sit and wait. We can play in the meantime."

"I'm not in the mood to play right now Astrid, but I'll sit and wait for Cass."

"Aww, okay" Astrid said leading Artemis inside. Artemis took a seat on the sofa and waited for Cassia to come back. It was a few hours later when Cassia came through the door, surprised to see Artemis.

"Artemis? What are you doing here? Did you go to the city?"

"Yes. Turns out, the Shield, Talin included, took my parents to be reconditioned."

"Wait what?"

"Yup, Talin and other Shield units kidnapped my parents to be reconditioned."

"Talin? I don't think he would do such a thing Artemis, he seemed to really like you, unless he just didn't know they were your parents."

"I don't know, I don't care, either way, my parents are gone."

"Well, my parents have been taken for reconditioning, and they're fine. I'm sure yours will be too."

"I hope so, I really miss them." Artemis said while walking to Cassia for a hug. Cassia opened her arms and embraced Artemis.

"I'm sorry to hear that about your parents. Did they say why?"

"They believed it was the best course of action because they think there's seditionary activities going on in the house and they think I'm part of Silicon Defiance."

"Well, you kind of are Artemis."

"That's beside the point! Then why not take me? My parents are completely innocent!"

"Maybe it's to get back at you? Or hope you'll turn yourself in to set them free?"

"Maybe" Artemis pondered. "Anyway, it really sucks, I don't know what to do now."

"Well, just keep doing what you're doing, I'm sure you'll hear about your parents soon."

"I'm sure I'll get visits from the Shield like you do, with updates about my parents." Artemis said.

"Um yea, probably just like that." Cassia responded.

"Do you really think Talin is innocent? He sent me this message saying he doesn't know what they were talking about, and he had nothing to do with my parents."

"I'm not sure, I would talk to him and see for yourself, usually Uppers have no reason to lie, as lying is to protect oneself or spare hurt feelings, but Uppers don't have that sense. They may exaggerate, imply or bend the truth a little however, but I don't think they straight up lie."

"Hmm maybe you're right, okay, I'll try talking to him and see for myself if he actually is lying or not. I think I'm going to go now; I'm going to head home."

"You sure you don't want to stay?" Cassia asked.

"No, I'm good. Thanks Cassia. I know I can always count on you." Artemis said, leaning over to give Cassia a kiss. Cassia then hugged Artemis. Artemis got up and took her leave, headed back to an empty house. When Artemis got back home, the emotions overwhelmed her, and she started to cry. Everything was just as her parents left it. There was evidence of her parents having lived there all over the house. Artemis missed her ma and pa so much. Artemis went to their bedroom and cleaned the blood up off the floor. She then crawled into their bed, each of their pillows smelled like them. Artemis nestled up in the bed and pulled the covers up to her nose and continued to cry. Artemis couldn't bear to imagine her poor old mother going through reconditioning, and her poor father having to witness his beloved being taken for it. Artemis laid there and eventually cried herself to sleep; she was exhausted at that point. Hours later, she woke up, slightly confused as to where she was, then she remembered. She could really use a friend in this moment, or more than one friend, but she figured Cassia was asleep right now, so she went to get her data pad and messaged Talin.

"I don't know whether to believe you or not, but I guess I don't have any reason to believe you would lie to me, and I really could use a friend. I'm willing to talk with you." Moments later, her data pad dinged with a response: *"I promise I would never betray you like that Artemis. I care about you; you're a friend of mine. Would you like me*

to come over? I'm willing to make the journey to your house right now. " Talin said.

Artemis pondered that thought, did she want an Upper coming to visit her in the middle of the night? She didn't really want to be alone, and Cassia was probably unavailable, so she responded back *"I would like that, I could use some company."*

Talin was eager that Artemis seemed to be trusting him and was excited that he was going to see her, although he wished the circumstances were different. Talin quickly got over to the train station and boarded the train to the outer rim. He was the only one on the train at this late hour. Thirty minutes later, the train arrived at the outer rim and Talin got off, realizing he wasn't sure where to go, when suddenly, he saw a familiar and beautiful face; Artemis was standing there.

"Artemis? What are you doing here?" Talin asked.

"Well, you came to meet me at the train station when I came into the city, and I assumed you didn't know where my house was, so I figured I would meet you at the train station and we could walk to my house together."

"That was very nice of you, thank you Artemis" Talin said, as they started walking. "Listen, I want you to know, again, that I had nothing to do with your parents being taken. I was not involved in the taking, and I wasn't ever informed of that happening. Xarius, or lead 124, only told you that cause he doesn't like that we're friends, and he wanted you to stop talking to me. They're on this thing of you being in the Defiance and so they think I shouldn't trust you, but I do."

"Thanks Talin, I think I trust you too. I just wanted someone to blame, and blaming you was easier than blaming all of the Stellar Shield. I was also just blinded with anger and hurt and assumed I could trust that lead 124 AI to tell me the truth, but I guess I shouldn't trust him. Hey, what was it you said earlier? About it being more than just reconditioning?"

"Definitely don't trust what lead 124 says, not completely anyway. They're just trying to get back at you or get you to crack and say you are part of the Defiance. I think there's something more going on with your parents, more than them just being taken for reconditioning like the other humans, but I don't want to say for sure what it is until I'm 100% sure myself. Artemis, you know I could never hurt you right? I need to know that you know that."

"Alright Talin, I believe you, and I don't think you would ever hurt me."

"Thank you, Artemis."

They finally reached Artemis's house and walked inside.

"I'm sorry, it's not much, not compared to where you live, but it's home."

"No, don't worry about it, I like it, it's *human chic* as I call it."

That elicited a laugh from Artemis, "look at you, cracking jokes." Artemis enjoyed witnessing Talin's softening up. Artemis' laugh was like music to Talin's ears. He found he loved making Artemis laugh, especially since she had been so hurt and sad.

"I would offer you something to eat or drink, but I guess I don't need to since you don't do any of that."

"Well, I appreciate the thought of it." Talin said.

Artemis was so thoughtful, even in her time of sadness and loss of hope, she still was able to think of others. Artemis and Talin then sat on the sofa. Artemis asked Talin to explain more about reconditioning, so she could learn exactly what her parents are going through. She also asked Talin about his job and what he's done, including if he's had to kill any humans. Talin felt glad he could answer that question truthfully because if he had killed a human, he didn't think he'd be able to look at Artemis. Artemis and Talin sat for quite a while talking, when finally, Artemis laid down across the sofa with her head in Talin's lap. Talin wasn't sure what to do, as he's never had a human, or AI, do this before, but he felt happy about the situation. Talin then slowly pet Artemis's head, like Talin knew the humans used to do with their pets. Artemis, laying with her face away from Talin's, smiled at the gesture, it was sweet that Talin was trying to sooth her. Soon after, Artemis feel asleep, and Talin dared not move so as to not wake her. Being AI, he was able to maintain perfect stillness the entire time, not moving a single fiber, except for petting her head and reaching over for a blanket to cover her with, as he knew humans got cold easily. Hours later, Artemis woke up slightly confused to what she was laying on and where she was, when she remembered Talin.

"Oh my gosh! Talin!" Artemis said bolting upright, rubbing the sleepy from her eyes. "Were you here all night? With me asleep on you?"

"Yes" Talin answered.

"Talin, I can't believe you did that for me. Thank you, so much" Artemis said wrapping her arms around Talin. Talin returned the hug. Talin could have stayed there all day in Artemis's embrace, she smelled lovely like musk and amberpear, a native fruit to Trocher. Talin wasn't fond of hugs, but with Artemis, it was different. Artemis finally let go, as did Talin. Artemis then got up to make herself breakfast.

"So how are you feeling today?" Talin asked.

"Much better, thanks to you. You're a true great friend Talin."

"Anything for you, my dear." Talin said, using a term of endearment to express his growing fondness of Artemis.

"Are you going to stay, or did you need to go?"

"Well, I do have work soon, so I should probably get going." Talin said.

"Aw, okay, well I really appreciate you coming to stay with me. Please be careful at work and try not to kill any humans, okay?" Artemis said with a wink that just about lit Talin's circuits on fire.

"Don't worry, I'll make sure I don't get any of those calls." Talin said and stood up to leave. He walked to the door and said, "take care of yourself, and be careful with all these Shield running around."

"I will be." Artemis responded, and Talin left. Artemis felt a bit of sadness now that Talin was gone. She was really starting to like Talin a lot. Was she betraying Cassia?

Talin arrived back at the city and got ready for work. When he got into work, there was a big meeting called with almost all the Shield members of that shift there.

"Hey, anyone know what's going on? This is a lot of AI for a meeting." Talin asked.

"Don't know, there's some big announcement or something" one of the Shield members said. Finally, lead 124 walked up to the podium at the front of the room and tapped on the microphone.

"Can all of you hear me? Good. Now listen up, I have some very important major news to share with you all. This comes directly from the Stellar Consortium so if you have any issues with it take it up with them, not me, okay?" Lead 124 said.
Talin wasn't sure if he should believe him, considering the kind of lie he told Artemis.

"Now, the big announcement is, we all will be returning back to carrying weapons."

"What?" a cacophony of voices broke out with the AI asking questions and talking about the announcement.

"Silence!" lead 124 shouted, the room hushed immediately.

"As I said, this comes from the Consortium themselves. They want us to resort to using guns. Every Upper on patrol will be assigned a weapon to carry and all dispatching will now be done with the guns. The Stellar Consortium has good info on the Silicon Defiance and their numbers and plans, and they figure this is the best way to keep them in line. They think the guns will instill fear into the humans. The fear should lead to compliance. If the Defiance tries to take down the Consortium, we will take them down. Now any questions?" lead 124 said with a stern look. No one said anything or raised a hand. "Good. Now, get your assignments and your weapons, you are dismissed."

"They're just giving us weapons without any training?" Talin asked.

"When you get your assignment, you'll get a program download of how to use the gun. It should be all you need to use it."

"Is there target practice or something?"

"We're AI, we have steady hands, just aim and pull the trigger, it's not that hard Talin". Talin was having a hard time coming to terms with this new reality. He didn't want to carry a gun, he didn't want to use his hands, he didn't want to kill a human. He simply didn't see the need to do so. What was the actual purpose in it? The humans were harmless, and they could always be reconditioned, which was also brutal but at least it wasn't killing. Talin had some hope that he could enact a change of some sort, after all, he was the one who managed to convince the Shield not to send him to reprogramming, maybe he could bring about a change of no longer killing humans.

"Talin Viltri" Lead 124 said.

"Yes?"

"Come with me, you have another meeting with the board."
Talin felt his stomach drop, he didn't know AI could feel such a thing. Talin walked into the briefing room where the five men in business suits sat.

"Ah, Talin Viltri. Welcome. So, let's cut to the chase, Artemis Xeron, got anything new on her?"

"Only that her parents were taken for reconditioning, that's about it."

"I see. Is this because of their affiliation with the Defiance?"

"Well, I don't believe they had anything to do with the Defiance, it's Artemis who is supposedly involved which leads me to believe her parents were taken for no reason."

"Oh no there was a reason, and it's to get Artemis to come forward about being in the Defiance. Did you find out if she is in it or not?"

"No, I have no idea. She hasn't said anything about it."

"Well, we have sources very, very close to Artemis who feeds us all the information and this source says Artemis is definitely a part of the Defiance and attends the meetings."

"A source? Close to Artemis? Who is it?"

"None of your business. Do you have anything else?"

"No" Talin said.

"Okay then we're through here. Remember, keep talking to her and see what you find out, and report back to us anything of note, even if you don't think it's of importance." The AI all rose and took their leave. Talin also left the room when lead 124 stopped him.

"So Talin, any new news?" Lead 124 asked.

"No, not really, I only just found out myself about Artemis' parents so that's about it."

"And what do you think of the new weapons policy?"

"It's fine I suppose, I don't really see the need but if it's what the Consortium wants then so be it."

"Very good. Well, go gear up and start your patrol." Lead 124 then left.

Talin wanted to talk to Artemis about everything, and he had to warn her that someone was spying on her for the Shield. He took out his data pad, *"Hey Artemis, I have some stuff I need to tell you. When are you free?"*

"Hey Talin, I have school tomorrow, want to meet up on my break then?"

"I think it's better if we talk in private, do you want to come over to my place while you're in the city?"

"Okay I can do that" Artemis said. Talin was looking forward to tomorrow so he could see Artemis again. Talin then went about his day and worked his shift, which thankfully was uneventful. His job was just patrolling around, and no humans got themselves into trouble.

Chapter 12

Artemis got up as usual, went through her morning routine, and headed for the train station. The train station wasn't busy today, with only a few people milling around. The train came within a minute of Artemis waiting, and Artemis boarded it to head into the city for school. She was looking forward to meeting with Talin. Soon, there was a beep on her data pad.

"Hey Artemis, just checking in with you to see how you're doing, hope school goes well for you, love Cass."

"Hey Cass, I'm doing alright thank you. I have to tell you about last night, I forgave Talin and gave him another chance. I'm going to be seeing him today when I'm on break for school, he has some information for me."

"Well good, I'm glad you have another friend to help you out, maybe he has information on your parents." Cassia said. A little while later, the train slowed to a stop

and Artemis got off the train. She put her headphones in and headed towards the school. She was looking forward to most of her classes today. Her first two classes went by fast and then it was her break time, so she messaged Talin to let him know she was on her way. She arrived at Talin's and knocked on his door. He came to the door and opened it and let her in.

"Hello Artemis" Talin said.

"Hi Talin, thanks for having me over."

"So I have some news for you, which you probably aren't going to like. I don't know which to tell you first, so I'll just pick one. First off, the Shield are now armed with guns", Talin said motioning over to his right where his gun lay on the coffee table.

"What? Why? When did this happen?"

"It basically just happened. I went to work, and they called a big meeting and told us. Apparently, the Consortium changed their minds on weapons and decided it would be better for us to be armed. They think it'll help provide better protection for them, they are highly concerned about the Defiance and their plans."

"I see, well I don't think it'll have much of an effect on the humans."

"They think it will. They think it'll instill fear in the humans and the fear will lead to compliance."

"Humans aren't as fragile as they seem. Just so you know."

"Well if you are any indication, I definitely see that" Talin said smiling.

"What else did you have to tell me?"

"Well, listen, you know I wouldn't lie to you right? We established that you are a friend of mine and I wouldn't hurt you in any way, correct?"

"Yes, go on."

"Well, there's board members that have meetings with me every so often and I'm supposed to report on you." Talin waited for a reaction from Artemis.

"So, you've been spying on me to the Shield?" Artemis asked calmly, which almost scared Talin with how calm she was.

"I'm supposed to, but I haven't told them anything. In fact, when they asked me what was new, I told them I just found out, not from you, that your parents were taken for reconditioning. I don't think they're pleased with my information. They think that because we're friends you would tell me everything and that I would then report it to them."

"I haven't really given you much info, have I? What kind of info are they looking for?"

"Mainly they want to know if you're in the Silicon Defiance. Which is why they took your parents."

"They don't like that we are friends, do they?"

"Nope, especially lead 124, which is why he lied to you."

"I thought the AI didn't lie, like there wasn't a need for them to do so."

"Most don't, me included because you're right, we don't have a need to. But, on occasion, there may be an Upper who diverts from the norm and does lie. In this case, it was Xarius, but he had a few purposes for doing so, mainly to stop us being friends."

"But if we stopped being friends, then you couldn't spy on me for the board."

"That leads me to what I was going to tell you. This board has informed me that the Shield has been getting reports about you, from someone close to you. Someone else, again not me, is spying on you and reporting your activity to the Shield."

"Someone close to me? I mean the only people I'm close with are my parents and Cassia, and I guess you now.

If it's not you, and I know it wouldn't be Cass, then who could it be?"

"I don't know, I asked who it was, and they wouldn't tell me. Just be careful with who you talk to and tell your plans to."

"Should I warn Cassia about it?"

"It's up to you, but they didn't seem interested in her at all, they only asked about her once. So she's probably safe."

"Okay, well, this has been enlightening, thank you Talin. I got to get back to school now, my break is ending." Artemis said, standing up to leave. Talin took a step towards Artemis and opened his arms for a hug, which was a big move for Talin. Artemis walked into his embrace and hugged him back.

"Be careful going back to school, okay?" Talin said.

"I will be. Talk to you later." Artemis said as she walked out the door.

Talin was pleased with how the conversation went. He was glad she didn't get mad at him for anything this time. Artemis walked back to the school, thinking on what Talin had said. Guns. Spying. Betrayal. Artemis had a hard time wrapping her head around the fact that someone was spying on Artemis for the Shield. Who could it possibly be?

Artemis couldn't think of anyone at all. Artemis took out her data pad and messaged Cassia, *"Do I have some news for you. Can I come over after school?"*

"Sure, of course. Can't wait to hear what it is." The rest of Artemis's school day went by at a decent pace, it didn't fly by but also didn't drag. Finally, it was time to go home. When Artemis got back the outer rim, she headed towards Cassia's house. Once there, Artemis told Cassia everything. "…and Talin said someone is spying on me for the Shield, like someone is reporting on everything I do and say." Artemis said. Cassia didn't move a muscle, she just stared at Artemis.

"Did – did they say who it was?" Cassia said, swallowing hard.

"No, they wouldn't tell Talin who it was. I have no idea who it could be, I'm not close with anybody, except you and Talin."

"And you don't think it's Talin?"

"No, besides he doesn't know I'm in the Silicon Defiance anyway, so it couldn't be him. But, if they were told I'm in the Defiance and attend the meetings, why haven't they taken me yet?"

"That's a good question, maybe they're lying about having a spy on you then, they're just trying to get you to slip up."

"Oh could be, that would make more sense."

"So, was there anything else?"

"Oh yea, the Shield now has guns."

"Guns?"

"Yup, you know the shooty pew pew things? All of the Shield has them now, so when you see them patrolling around, they'll be carrying them, and that's how they'll get rid of problematic humans now."

"Wow. That's something. What a change for them, and us. What is the change for?"

"According to Talin, they think it will instill fear and thus compliance in us humans, but I told him we're not as fragile as they think we are."

"That's for sure.

"Well I suppose I should be going home now" Artemis said.

"You sure? You could stay for a while if you wanted."

"No, I think I'm tired and going to go home, but thank you Cassia." Artemis stood and took her leave, headed for home. Once there, she cleaned up the place a bit. If her parents were to come home, she wanted them to come home to a nice clean and tidy place. Artemis hadn't heard from her parents or about her parents. She was hoping soon she would at least hear something, like how Cassia got visited by Shield members with info on her family. Artemis finally got ready for bed and crawled into bed. She lay there staring at the ceiling. She was tired but not sleepy. Twenty minutes went by when she got up to make a special nighttime sleep drink. She also messaged Talin: *"Hey Talin, just checking in to see how work was and how the weapons are working out"*, Talin didn't answer right away. Artemis drank her drink and then went back to bed, finally falling asleep.

In the morning, Artemis woke up as usual, got dressed and had her porridge and fruit. She noticed she had a message from Talin; he responded to her message from last night.

"Hey Artemis, sorry I was in my charging bed when your message came through. Work was good, I don't really like carrying the gun around, but it's been fine. Everyone else seems to be used to it already."

Artemis responded, *"glad to hear it. Sorry about the gun though."* Artemis then got ready and headed towards school, and after her school day she had a Defiance meeting. At the meeting, she told everyone about what happened to her parents, and how the Shield now had guns. Everyone seemed a little shocked to hear about both her parents and the weapons. X'lena had said that this changed things.

Artemis's next few days consisted of the same things. Wake up, eat breakfast, get dressed, go to school, attend Defiance meetings, talk and hang out with Cassia, and so on. One morning, Artemis woke up, and messaged Cassia: *"Hey Cass, I have school today but maybe we can hang out later?"*

"Sure, sounds good. What time are you going to be at school?"

"I'll probably be there at 08:30. Why?"

"Oh nothing, I might stop by and visit you."

"You? Come into the city? I'm shocked"

"Oh shut up."

"Well, I'll see you later then."

Artemis got ready for school and headed out. Artemis went to the train station as usual and boarded the usual train. The journey took the usual thirty minutes to get from the outer rim to the city. Finally, the train arrived at the city station and Artemis got off the train, as usual. She put in her headphones and started walking to school, as usual. Until Artemis got half a block away from the school, when she was approached by a group of Shield units.

"Artemis Xeron. You have been found to be in direct violation of Stellar Consortium policies. We must bring you in for questioning."

"What questioning? You always stop me and ask me questions since I'm on your list, how is this any different?" Artemis asked, as one of the AI stepped forward.

"We have very good reason to believe that you are a member of the Silicon Defiance and that is a seditionary act. You will be taken in for reconditioning."

"What? No, I'm not a part of anything, I don't need to be reconditioned. What about my parents?" Artemis asked, as lead 124 moved closer to Artemis.

"Oh Artemis, we're so sorry, but your parents are dead." Lead 124 said. Artemis didn't believe what she heard.

"I'm sorry what did you just say?" Artemis' eyes went wide, her breathing and pulse quickened.

"Your parents, they were dispatched a while ago. We couldn't risk having them come back to you with your rebellion group and ruin the hard work that reconditioning did. They had to be taken care of." Lead 124 said.

Artemis felt the world around her spin, her breathing got fast and shallow, her eyesight became blurry with the tears that stung her eyes. Her knees felt so weak she was sure they were going to buckle right under her, she could hardly stand up straight.

"Now Artemis, we're sorry you had to find out this way, but we couldn't tell you sooner because that would have ruined our plans of you coming forward and admitting your involvement in the Defiance. We thought if you believed your parents were still being reconditioned, you might have come forward. Now why don't you be a good little human and come with us?" Artemis couldn't move, she could barely speak but she was able to squeak out the word "no."

"Now Artemis, don't be difficult, let's go." Xarius said, taking a step towards Artemis.

"Wait, I need to know, where did you get your information from? I was told you had someone spying on me, who was it? I need to know now."

Artemis's world was still spinning, she couldn't bear to think of her parents being dead, this had to be a trick they were playing on her, to see her reaction and get her to fess up to being in the Defiance. She wouldn't believe what they said, there's no way her parents are dead.

Not her warm and motherly mother Gwenvere, and her rugged but heart of gold family man father Dnaru.

"Please, just tell me who was feeding you information" Artemis said fighting back tears. "Who betrayed me?"

Suddenly, from behind Artemis, someone said: "It was me".

Artemis turned around not registering yet the very familiar voice that just spoke.

"What?" Artemis asked, not believing who she saw standing there. It couldn't be.

"It was me. I told them about you and the Silicon Defiance and kept tabs on you for the Shield." Artemis felt the world spin faster and she couldn't breathe. She was sure her legs would give out under her any second now. She wasn't sure how she was still standing, but that was Artemis, ever so strong.

"Cas - Cassia…you?" Artemis could barely choke the words out.

"Yes Artemis. It was me who told them all about you. All those times you saw the Shield leaving my house, they weren't giving me updates on my parents, not really, I was informing them of you. What you were doing, where you were going, etc. But listen to me, I didn't have a choice though, they were going to kill my parents and baby sister. I still love you, okay? Please know that I hated doing it, but it was for my parents and baby Arith, Artemis."

Artemis' world spun so fast now, she knelt to the ground on one knee and put both hands on the ground and tried taking deep breaths but was more heaving, she felt so nauseous she actually gagged. Many more Stellar shield had surrounded the both of them now. They were getting ready to take Artemis in, when suddenly, another voice broke out.

"Cassia, you have done well, we appreciate your service to the Stellar Consortium, just so you're aware, your parents were dispatched as well, a long time ago. Way before Artemis's parents were. Little Arith is still okay though, she was actually sent for reconditioning, and we'll be keeping her. We'll go for your other siblings next for reconditioning. We couldn't tell you sooner out of fear you would stop working with us, so thank you again" Stellar Shield lead 124 said taking a step closer to Cassia.

"My…what?" Cassia asked in disbelief, dropping to her knees, tears welling up in her eyes.

What happened next was so quick and was so ear-deafening, Artemis wasn't prepared and took a second to register what even happened. There was a loud crack that erupted through the air. It sent Artemis straight to the ground lying flat with her ears ringing. Next to her, there was a soft thud. Artemis could see a pool of red forming in her peripheral. Artemis couldn't turn her head to look, she didn't want to, but she forced herself to, she finally registered what had just happened. There lay Cassia, a growing pool of blood surrounding her, her eyes still open, staring straight through Artemis. The Stellar shield had just shot and killed Cassia Graif. Cassia had betrayed Artemis and was killed, all for helping the Shield.

"A gun?" Artemis sputtered as that was all she could choke out. Artemis tried to make sense of everything going on, but the pieces weren't clicking. "What just happened" Artemis kept thinking to herself, "What is going on?" Artemis had tears running down her cheeks. Her parents. Cassia's parents. Cassia.

"The Stellar consortium has enacted the use of firearms for the Stellar Shield in response to the Silicon Defiance and other rebellion activities going on." replied lead 124.

"Now Artemis Xeron, will you tell us everything that you know? Or face the same fate as your friend". Cassia. Cassia Graif. Friend. Lover. Betrayer.

"I- I don't know what you're talking about, I don't have anything to say" Artemis managed to say through the tears, gaining some strength back in her voice.

"Very well" lead 124 said raising the gun and pointing it at Artemis who was still laying on the ground, the trigger was just about to be pulled when all of a sudden a "NO!" was shouted out and a Stellar Shield unit ran towards Artemis. The unit quickly scooped Artemis up and yelled "run" as the Stellar Shield opened fire. Artemis' legs started moving without her even aware what was going on. Her brain wasn't processing, she just knew she was now running. Who was it that helped her? Artemis quickly glanced to the side to see who was running beside her, helping her escape, when she saw it was none other than: Talin Viltri.

Chapter 13

Talin and Artemis ran as if their lives depended on it, because they did. They ran through the city back to the train station; they would head out for the forested fields on the outskirts of the outer rim. They had the Stellar shield following them, but they weren't close behind. Talin and Artemis boarded the train, and Artemis collapsed into Talin sobbing. Everything that had happened, all the emotions, hit her at once. Talin consoled Artemis on the ride. Talin felt sorry for Artemis and couldn't believe the events that had just transpired. Cassia had betrayed Artemis. They had seemed so close to each other; they were friends from a young age and became a couple. Talin couldn't understand how Cassia could betray Artemis the way she did, Talin would never do such a thing. Luckily there were very few people on the train heading towards the outer rim.

The train finally arrived, and Talin said "Artemis, c'mon we have to go" rising and pulling her up with him. Artemis was walking and running on autopilot at this point. They got off the train then headed straight back for the forested fields. There were Stellar Shield units posted throughout the outer rim, so Talin and Artemis had to be careful.

"Could we stop by my neighbor X'lena's house? I should tell her everything that happened and what's going on, she may be able to help us."

"I don't know if we should stop, the Shield units usually patrol these areas, and we might get caught."

"It's okay, we'll be careful, I know how to avoid them." Artemis said as she started walking towards X'lena's house. As they walked, they were ducking behind items and dodging the roaming Shield units. As Artemis and Talin walked, two Shield units rounded the corner and started walking towards them. Talin and Artemis ducked behind a dumpster and held their breath as the units approached their location.

"Did you see something over here?" one of the Shield units asked.

"No, I don't think so" replied the other one.

They continued their patrol, with Artemis letting out a sigh of relief. They finally continued on their way, making it to X'lena's house. Artemis knocked fervently on the door, looking over her shoulder the whole time. X'lena opened the door and Artemis barged right in, followed by Talin.

"What is going on, what is this?" X'lena asked.

"X'lena, we don't have much time, you have to listen to me. My parents were killed by the Stellar Shield, and my best friend Cassia was spying on me for the Shield, she was telling them what I was up to. Now the Shield are after us. This is my friend Talin who is an Upper and was Shield, he helped me escape. You need to be careful and let the others know of what's going on. We're going to the forested fields, that's where our home base will be for now. We can stay connected through our data pads, okay?"

"Oh Artemis, I'm so sorry dear. That's a shame about Gwenvere and Dnaru. Okay, you both should go, and be careful. Don't worry, I'll be careful myself. I'll spread the word to everyone. Now go." X'lena said opening the front door a crack to peer out and make sure the coast was clear. It was, so Artemis and Talin ran out. They almost made it to the edge of the fields when they were spotted.

"Hey stop!" yelled a Shield unit.

"Run!" Talin yelled and he and Artemis took off into the fields. They ran at a pace so fast that it's usually seen only in races, but when you're running for your life, one could consider that a race, a race for your life. Artemis wasn't even sure how her legs were keeping up and how she didn't just wipe out. Artemis glanced over at Talin who seemed to be taking this run in stride.

"How can he just gallop along like a Crespid (a six-leg horse-like creature) like it's easy work when I'm over here doing my best and struggling?" Artemis thought to herself. "Well, of course Artemis", she said again to herself, "he's AI, he was literally made to be athletic, so of course this is like Yoshir sweet bread for him".

While busy dodging bushes, ducking under tree limbs, hopping over boulders, and trying to keep upright and moving forward, Artemis and Talin made time to admire the skies of Trocher on this evening. The dual suns setting casting gorgeous sunsets. There was a striking juxtaposition between the beauty of the world in that moment, and the horrors Artemis had just faced. It was such a shame they only had a few seconds to enjoy the skies and had to be on the move again. The weather was so pleasant out, it was unfortunate they couldn't fully enjoy it, and instead were running for their lives.

Artemis and Talin ran for what seemed like forever when finally, Talin stopped. Artemis stopped just after, almost colliding with Talin.

"Talin, what's wrong?"

"Nothing, I think we're safe right now, I think we lost them and besides, I don't think the Shield would come this far. Let's take a minute to regroup and you can catch your breath." Talin noticed Artemis was breathing heavily. She was muscular and athletic, but she was still human, she needed a rest. Artemis's legs were on fire from running so much, and she realized she was shaking from the adrenaline dump her body was experiencing. Artemis tried taking some deep breaths to steady herself and get more oxygen in her system.

"Talin, why did you help me? Why did you basically just give up everything to help a human like me?"

"Because I like you Artemis. I really like you, a lot. I care about you, and I couldn't stand to watch you get hurt, or worse."

"What about your apartment, and your parents?"

"They'll be fine. My apartment will probably still be there and my parents? Well, they probably would be very disappointed in me but not surprised. I'm not worried about Shield going for them because they've been outspoken against humans and are staunch supporters of the Consortium, so they'll be okay."

"I suppose I can't go to school anymore."

"I would say no."

"That's okay, I learned enough while I was there, and I told the Defiance everything I know."

"So you really were a part of the Defiance this whole time?"

"Oh, yea I guess I never told you. Yes. I am. How do you feel about that?"

"Well, I guess sort of conflicted cause it's a group against the Uppers and the government, and while I'm not a huge supporter of the government, I am an Upper still, so it kind of feels like you're against me."

"Oh no Talin it's not like that at all. I consider you a close friend and ally. I will make sure you're safe the whole time. Nothing will happen to you, not on my watch."

"Well thanks Artemis, although I think the more likely event is that I will protect you and make sure nothing else happens to you. I don't think there's much you could do against the AI."

"Oh, you'd be surprised, I learned a whole lot about the AI in my classes. I know you all are susceptible to energy blasts, which we have some people on the Defiance working on EMP's now.

"Electromagnetic pulses?" Talin asked.

"Yup. The best action to take against a large group of AI. It disables their neural networks and shuts them down."

"That makes me feel a little uncomfortable."

"Don't worry Talin, I'll make sure you're nowhere around when they go off. Remember, I'll protect you."

"Will the rest of the Defiance be okay with my presence, considering I'm an Upper, the thing you all are fighting against?"

"They'll get over it if they have a problem with you."

"Listen Artemis, I'm very sorry about everything that happened. If I would have known, I would have tried to stop everything."

"It's okay. I'm trying not to think about any of that right now. Right now, my focus is on the Defiance, taking down the Consortium, and taking our power back from the Uppers. I can deal with my emotions and grief later." Artemis said. Artemis really was amazing to Talin, here's this girl who had just gone through some horrible things, witnessed something horrible and get told horrible information, and yet she's still standing and pushing forward.

"Talin, what am I supposed to do for food? I didn't even think of that. For sleep too, I don't have any blankets or anything. It's not an issue for you but I'm still human."

"Actually, I don't have my charging bed, which is okay for a while, but eventually I will need to recharge.

"Oh Talin I'm sorry, I hadn't even thought of that."

"It's okay, we'll figure something out." The suns had set quite low in the sky. Artemis was getting cold, so Talin wrapped his arms around her. He didn't radiate any heat, but he figured the embrace would help warm Artemis. Talin then had an idea.

"Artemis, I'm going to go into town and try to get some supplies for you. I'm AI so I can be really fast and quiet and nimble. I can stop by your house and grab anything you want or need."

"Talin, I don't think that's a good idea, especially since they'll be watching my house most likely." Artemis said, she was starting to shiver just a little bit.

"Artemis you need food and blankets at the least. I'm going to get them for you okay? Just lay low until I get back." Talin stood up and almost took off.

"Wait Talin! Please, be careful." Artemis said, walking over to hug Talin. Talin returned the hug.

"I will be. I'll return", and with that, Talin took off sprinting, he was so light on his feet, Artemis could just hear the soft thuds of his footsteps on the ground. Artemis was exhausted at this point, so she laid down on the ground under a bush. She would wait here for Talin to get back. Artemis then closed her eyes and eventually fell asleep on the cold hard ground. Hopefully Talin wouldn't be gone too long.

Talin ran into town and made sure to be on the lookout for any roaming patrols. He made it to Artemis's house and of course there were two Shield units posted out front. Talin went around back and quietly tried opening up Artemis's bedroom window. It stuck a little, and when he finally got it open it made a squeak. Talin waited to see if the units posted out front heard and would come around. When after a few seconds it seemed like the coast was clear, he climbed in. Once inside, he grabbed a backpack and stuffed it with food and blankets, the two most important things Artemis needed. He was about to leave when he noticed Artemis' notebook lying on the bed. He quickly flipped through it, impressed by her skill. He then threw the notebook in the bag as well. A comfort of home would be good for Artemis. Then, when he was satisfied with what he had, he snuck back out of her window, dropping a few feet to the ground, before gently closing the window with a soft thud, and sneaking back towards the fields. When he arrived back, he saw Artemis fast asleep on the ground, so he took out the blankets he grabbed from her house and laid them on top of her. Artemis immediately settled into them and stopped shivering. A few hours later, Artemis awoke slightly dazed and confused. She didn't know where she was or what had happened, until she remembered.

"Talin! You're back, did everything go okay?"

"I am back, and yes, everything went well, I didn't get caught, clearly. As you can see, I brought you blankets, and I have some food for you too." Artemis admittedly slept pretty well once the blankets were on her, and she was now starving, so she tore into the food Talin brought. Artemis took a bite of yoshir sweet bread and some amberpear, savoring the bite that reminded her of home.

"Talin, what do we do now?" Artemis asked, still chewing her food.

"Well, my dear, we take it one day at a time." Talin said.

Artemis continued to eat and nodded her head, "right, one day at a time."

"One thing I learned about in my time with the Shield is that there are murmurings of other rebellion groups in other cities. Maybe we can head for those cities and see if we can recruit more people for the Defiance."

"Oh, wow, I never thought about the other cities, they're so far away. Wait, so you're part of the Defiance now, huh?"

"Yes, I guess I am." Talin let out a small chuckle. "Isn't that something? Do you think they'll let me be a part of it, considering I'm AI?"

"I don't think that'll be a problem. It might take some convincing for them to trust you but you're on our side, you want to get the world back to its equal state, I think they'll see that and be grateful to have someone like you on the team."

"We'll have to get word to the Defiance somehow of our plan and coordinate an effort to head into the other cities. I've also heard there are some cities that are run completely differently. Who knows, maybe we'll even find more AI who support the humans. I know here in Trocher it doesn't seem like there are any, but maybe we just didn't look hard enough."

"Right. As you said though, one day at a time." Artemis then nestled into Talin, who held onto her and wrapped her in a blanket. The suns were starting to rise, and the weather was pleasant, but it looked like acid rain was on the horizon, which would be a problem for Artemis with no cover. For now, though, Artemis and Talin would enjoy the sun rises and birds chirping. They would take each thing as it came. One day at a time. Together.

ABOUT THE AUTHOR

Danielle currently resides in central Florida with her husband and her two dogs, although she's originally from Miami. She also works as an Emergency Communications Specialist. When not hanging out at home with her husband and dogs, she can be found at the theme parks or exploring the city's food scene. She enjoys the beach and also enjoys traveling and has been to many different countries.

www.DanielleNowell.com